U0620479

从经典作家进入历史

希尼在都柏林桑迪芒特码头，一九九六年
（Bobbie Hanvey 摄，Sandymount Pier, Dublin）

希尼出生于北爱尔兰德里郡。他的第一本诗集
《一个博物学家之死》初版于一九六六年，后
又出版了诗歌、批评和翻译作品，使他成为他
那一代诗人中的翘楚。一九九五年，他获得诺
贝尔文学奖；两度荣获惠特布莱德年度图书奖
（《酒精水准仪》，1996；《贝奥武甫》，1999）。
由丹尼斯·奥德里斯科尔主持的访谈录《踏脚
石》出版于二〇〇八年；他的最后一本诗集《人
之链》获得二〇一〇年度前瞻诗歌奖最佳诗集
奖。二〇一三年，希尼去世。他翻译的维吉尔
《埃涅阿斯纪》第六卷在其去世后出版（2016），
赢得批评界盛誉。

◇中英双语版◇

幻视

酒精水准仪

[爱尔兰] 谢默斯·希尼 著 朱玉 译

广西师范大学出版社
·桂林·

幻　视

1991

给德里克·马洪

目录

致　谢

　　本集中的一些诗最初发表在以下报刊上，谨向这些报刊的编辑致谢：《备忘录》《阿耆尼评论》《安泰》《贝尔法斯特通讯报》《英语评论》《田野》《佐治亚评论》《爱尔兰时报》《伦敦书评》《观察者》《环球》《猫头鹰》《牛津公报》《牛津诗歌》《帕纳索斯》《犁铧》《爱尔兰诗歌》《诗歌评论》《大杂烩》《保留》《星期日论坛报》《泰晤士诗刊》《三便士评论》《泰晤士报文学增刊》《救赎》《翻译》。

　　以下诗歌最初发表在《纽约客》：《一篮栗子》，《穿越》第 xviii, xxx, xxxi, xxxii, xxxiii, xxxiv, xxxv, xxxvi 首。

　　第一部分中的许多诗歌曾收录于诗集《树钟》（亚麻厅图书馆，贝尔法斯特，1990）。

金 枝

（《埃涅阿斯纪》，第六卷，第 98–148 行）

于是库迈的西比尔从她的圣坛后

唱出可怖的模糊词语，回荡整个山洞

清晰的真理和神秘的事情不可分割地

缠绕在她话中。阿波罗朝着她的胸

旋转马刺，让她清醒，控制了她的发作。

她的癫狂刚消失，疯言疯语刚停止

英雄埃涅阿斯就开口："没有考验，哦，女祭司，

你想象不出有任何考验会让我震惊

因为我已预见并预先承受过一切。

但我只祈求一件事：因为他们说

此地能找到通往冥府之王的入口，

阿刻戎冥河从幽暗的沼泽汹涌流过，

我只求看一眼，面对面看看我亲爱的父亲。

指教我那路线并敞开神圣的门。

我曾用这双肩膀背负他走出战火

和敌人成千上万的长矛。激烈的战斗中我救下他

与他并肩度过我所有的海上漂泊，

一位老者，饱经风霜却坚强不屈。

也正是他一半请求一半命令我

来与你商谈，找到你并请求你，

所以，贞洁的女祭司，我请求你垂怜

一对父子，因为没有什么不在你的掌控中，

正因如此赫卡忒命你看管茂密的阿佛纳斯。

如果俄耳甫斯能召回他妻子的亡魂

凭借他对色雷斯竖琴嘹亮悦音的信心，

如果波吕克斯能赎回一位兄弟

凭借轮流频繁往返于死亡之地，

如果忒修斯也能，还有伟大的赫拉克利斯……但

　为什么说起他们？

我的出身最高贵，朱庇特的后人。"

他那样祈求着，坚守在祭坛边

这时女先知开始说话："诸神的血亲，

特洛伊人，安喀塞斯之子，通往阿佛纳斯的路简单。

幽冥之王普鲁托的门昼夜开放。

但要原路返回上面的空间，

这才是真正艰巨的任务。

少数人做到了，诸神的儿子们，

被正义的朱庇特所偏袒，或在

雄壮的光芒中升天。森林覆盖在下界的中途，

叹息河在幽冥中蜿蜒，舔舐两岸。

不过，如果爱如此折磨你且你如此需要

两度驶过阴森的冥湖并两度审视

塔尔塔罗斯的幽暗，如果你一定要越过界限，

你该事先知道你必须做好准备。

在一棵浓密的树间隐藏着一根黄金做的树枝

它的叶子和柔韧的嫩枝也是金的。

对于下界的庇护人朱诺来说，它是圣物，

它被树丛遮盖着，重重深影积聚在

林木茂密的山谷。从来没有人获准

下到大地的隐秘处，除非他首先

从树上摘下这根金色羽翼的枝条

交给美丽的普罗瑟皮娜，它的合法

拥有者，属于她的特殊礼物。当它被摘下，

它的位置永远会长出另一枝来，依然是金的，

在它上面生长的叶子拥有同样的金属光泽。

因此，抬头看，仔细找，当你找到它，

勇敢无误地抓住它。如果命里注定，

金枝总会容易取下，心甘情愿跟你走。

否则，无论你使多大劲，你都无法

征服它或割下它，哪怕用最锋利的刀刃。”

第一部分

归　途

拉金的幽魂让我一惊。他援引但丁：

"白昼将尽，赭色的空气
抚慰大地上每一个生灵，
将他们从各处的劳作中释放。

只有我准备好独自面对
旅途与义务的艰巨考验
一切都没有改变，如高峰期的巴士

载着疲惫负重的人们穿过城市。
我本应是一位贤明的君王
在圣诞彩灯下启程——只是

这更像一场被预先告诫的归途
回归日常事务的中心地带。
还是我原来的自己。准备喝一杯酒。

一个朝九晚五、见过诗歌的人。"

标　记

一

我们标记球场：四件夹克做四个门柱，
这就是全部。四角和方格
在长满蓟花的崎岖土地下
如同经度和纬度，必要时
人们会谈判，同意或者
不同意。然后我们挑选队友，
根据点到的名字跨过界线。

少年们在球场上喊破了头，
天色逝去，他们还玩个不停，
因为那时他们在想象中踢球，
而真正被踢的球到来时
如沉甸甸的梦，夜色中他们
粗重的呼吸和草地上的跌跤
听起来恍若另一世界的努力……
这一切短暂而持久，一场无须
发生的游戏。某种界限被越过，
在加长、难料、自由的时间里
有一种敏捷、向前和不知疲倦。

你也爱花园里木桩标出的界线，

铁锹沿着拉紧的白绳划出

第一道笔直的边界。或伸展的绳子

完美标划房屋地基的轮廓，

苍白的板条为每一个角落

标出直角，每一块新锯下的新板

整洁地躺在异常顺服的草丛。

或一道想象的线笔直划过

放牧的田野，等待被开垦，

从田垄一端的木桩到

另一端的木桩。

三

　　　　所有这些事进入你

仿佛它们既是门也是穿过门的东西。

它们标记地点、标记时间并保持敞开。

割草机切分青铜麦海。

辘轳从水中拖出中心。

两人拉一把横锯，让它来回

游刃于一棵倒下的山毛榉，

仿佛他们在划动稳固的大地之舟。

三幅素描

1. 得 分

那些日子——
把一个皮足球踢得
更真更远
超出你的预期!

球骨碌骨碌
势不可当
滚过雏菊和千里光,
它重击

但也唱歌,
一种即将消逝的
干涩、响亮的声音。
或者,巧妙的传球

和边线的喝彩
"射门!"球弹起,
不可阻挡的绝杀!
是你

还是球一直跑

在你前面，惊人地

越来越高

且可哀地自由？

2. 脉 动

旋转钓线
毫不费力。手腕
轻轻一挥，
鱼饵就快速漾开，

喃喃地，丝滑地，
轻巧地坠着。
看上去就是浮起
并发光，完全不是

难事——只是纯粹的
持续，结束时，
钓线在水中
发出的脉动

在你手掌中
比记忆里小鸟的心跳
还要轻。然后，在全部
释放后，你感到欢欣

当你收线并发现

自己被串连，从脚尖

到竿尖，连入河流

稳固的紧握与轰鸣。

3. 渔 获

从托尔和巨人希米尔①
那里跑掉的
正是世界巨蟒。
神在他的钓线上

挂牛头作诱饵，旋转抛高
又投入大海深处。
但这场大捕捞突然终止，
因为托尔的脚踩破了甲板，

希米尔吓得用切诱饵的刀
切断鱼线。然后
翻滚，骚动，震荡！
一条银河出现在水上。

他在船上击穿的洞
裂开，就像托尔的头
在大海上裂开。

———————————
① 托尔（Thor），北欧神话中的雷神。希米尔（Hymer），北欧
神话中的巨人。本诗演绎了托尔和希米尔一起钓鱼的故事。(本
书脚注皆为译者注)

他感到与时空合一，

失去屋顶，暴露无遗——
他空空的臂弯令他惊诧
像某个非凡的高空接球手
落空没接到球。

抛线与收线

给泰德·休斯

很多很多年以前，这些声音各执一词：

左岸，一条渐细的绿丝线
沙沙穿过空气，诉说静谧
与茂密，无拘无束，无论
掠过干草地还是河流。

右岸，像一只加速的长脚秧鸡，
尖锐的齿轮声持续、持续，
划破寂静，是另一个
垂钓者正把鱼线收回线盘。

我依然站在那里，清醒而梦幻，
我年纪大了，能看到他们俩
移动手臂和鱼竿，忙碌不停，
每个人都投入，被各自制造的声音屏蔽。

一个声音说，"你不值两便士，
但谁都不值。小心点！严肃点。"

另一个说,"顺其自然!随机应变,
你是你在河边感受的一切。"

我爱静谧的空气。我相信对立。
很多很多年过去了,我不转移,
因为我看见一个抛线,另一个收线,
反之亦然,无须交换场地。

父与子

一

"先抓老的,"
(我父亲的笑话同样老、沉重
且可预料。)"然后小的
都会跟来,就这么简单。"

在那些和缓明媚的河畔傍晚,甜蜜的时光
让他担心我们把太多事看作理所当然
因此我们的情绪必须受到轻微约束。

感恩脚踏实地!感恩高光时刻!
感恩那无言之爱的淡泊,
它来自那宽背、矮小的男人,
他一生怕欠债,但不时能
激起水花,像他说起的鲑鱼
"听声音足有小猪那么大。"

二

鲑鱼跳回水里,穿过它自己

无声的同心声波，在水潭的听力范围内，
割草匠永远倚着他的镰刀。

他把自己割到田野中央
站在最后那个完美的圆圈
阳光下收割后的麦田。

"去告诉你父亲，"割草匠说
（他对我父亲说，父亲告诉我）
"我把地割得精光，像一枚崭新的六便士。"

我父亲是捎信的赤脚男孩，
奔跑时目光同野草与禾束一样高
在他父亲死去的那个下午。

半扇门那半开着的漆黑等候着。
我感到空气里弥漫着焦灼与匆忙。
我感到远方他迅疾的脚步

莫名如我自己的——当他有朝一日
把我高高扛起，头晕，孱弱，
像一个从火中救出的痴呆老人。

幻　视

一

星期天早晨的伊尼什博芬岛。

阳光，炭烟，海鸥，船位，柴油。

一个接着一个，我们被送到

一条小船上，每次，船都可怕地

下沉并摇晃。我们三三两两

紧张地坐在短凳上，一动不动，

顺从，第一次挨得这么近，没有人说话，

除了船夫，当舷缘开始下沉

仿佛随时可能从舷侧进水。

大海风平浪静，但即便如此，

当发动机启动，我们的摆渡人

摇摆着保持平衡，将手伸向舵柄，

我为船体自身的动荡和重量

感到恐慌。确保我们安全的事物——

迅速的反应、浮力和漂流——

让我感到痛苦。从始至终

当我们平稳航行，横渡

深邃、平静、清澈见底的海水，

仿佛我从另一条航行在空中的船里

往下看，那么高，能看见

我们多么冒险地驶入那个早晨，

徒劳地爱着我们裸露、低垂、余日无多的头。

二

Claritas①。这不动感情的拉丁文

完美适用于石雕中的水

耶稣站在水里，水不及膝，

施洗约翰正往他头上倾泻

更多的水：这一切在明亮的阳光下，

在一座大教堂的正面。线条

坚硬，纤细而蜿蜒不断，代表

流动的河水。下方线条之间

稀奇的小鱼穿梭。别无他物。

然而在那极致的可见物里

石头中涌动着不可见之物：

水草，被搅扰而匆匆逝去的流沙，

以及如影、无影的溪水本身。

整个下午，灼热在台阶上摇曳

我们伫立时，眼前的空气摇曳

像代表生命的之字形象形文字。

———————————

① claritas：清晰，明朗。

三

从前，我那差点被淹死的父亲

走进我们的院子。他刚刚到河岸上的

田地里给土豆喷药去了

而且不带我去。马力喷洒机

太大太时新，蓝矾可能

灼伤我的眼睛，那匹马是新马，我

可能会吓到它，等等。我朝着

茅屋顶上的小鸟丢石子，不过是

为了听听石子的咔嗒声，

但是当他回来时，我在屋里

见他在窗外，眼神涣散，

惊慌，奇怪地没戴帽子，

脚步不稳，惊魂未定。

原来，当他在河岸上转弯时，

马受了惊，向后仰起，掀翻

马车、喷洒机和所有东西，失去平衡，

整套装备都跌进深深的

旋涡，马蹄，锁链，车辕，车轮，木桶

和工具，全都滚落到河里，

而那顶帽子已然欢乐地漂在

更安静的河段。那天下午

我面对面地看着他，他走来，
留下从河水中带来的湿脚印，
从那以后，我们之间再没有
什么令人不愉快的事情了。

枴　杖

他再也无法起身但他准备就绪。
走进来，像清晨时分的镜子，
他凝望巨大的窗外，出神，
不关心这天晴朗还是多云。

从楼上俯瞰整片地区。
第一批运奶车，第一缕烟，牛群，树木
潮湿而茂盛，在潮湿的树篱上空——
他独享这一切，像一个哨兵

被人忘记也无法记起
他究竟为了什么驻守高处，
释然醒来但仍在原地，
解脱，如一朵击碎的浪花。

当他的头越来越轻，他消瘦的手
绝望地摸索并找到枴杖这幻肢，
握在手中，让他安稳。
现在他找回他的触感，能坚守他的立场

或挥舞手杖如挥舞银枝并再度

走在我们中间：有名的裁判。

我本可以用树篱雕刻一个更好的伙计！

上帝可能说过同样的话，当他想起亚当。

一九八七年一月一日 ^①

危险的人行道。

但今年我用我父亲的手杖

应对寒冰。

一个八月的夜晚

他的手温暖，瘦小，历尽沧桑。

昨夜当我再次看见那双手，它们是两只雪貂，

独自嬉戏在月光下的田野。

视 野

我记得这个女人，长年
坐着轮椅，目光直直地
望向窗外的梧桐，落叶、
生叶，在远远的小巷尽头。

目光径直越过角落里的电视，
发育不良、狂躁的山楂树丛，
同样矮小的牛犊背朝风雨，
同样那片千里光，同样的山。

她坚定，就像那扇大窗本身。
她的额头光亮如椅上的合金。
她从不哀伤，也从不
怀有一点多余的情感负担。

与她面对面是一种教育
如同穿过一道坚固的铁门——
路边简单、干净、铁制的那种，
在两根白石灰柱间，从那里

你把这片地域看得更深，超出预期
并且发现树篱后面的田野
更加明显地陌生，当你一直伫立
聚焦并被那挡住道路的所吸引。

干草叉

在所有农具中，干草叉
最接近一种想象的完美：
当他握紧举起的手用它瞄准，
它就像标枪，精准而轻快。

所以不管他扮演勇士还是健儿，
或在干草和汗水中热忱劳作，
他都爱这根在自然打磨中变得丝滑的梣木，
爱它尖尖的斑驳的木柄上的纹理。

铆接的钢，车削的木，抛光，纹路，
平滑，笔直，圆润，修长，生辉。
汗浸的，磨利的，平衡的，检验的，合适的，
它的柔韧、轻快和冲刺。

然后当他想要刺探最远处，
他会看到干草叉的长柄
平稳而冷静地驶过空间，
它的尖齿映着星辉且寂然无声——

但他最终学会追随那简单的起航，
掠过它本来的目标，去往另一边，
在那里，完美——或近乎完美——被想象，
不在于瞄准而在于放开的手掌。

一篮栗子 [①]

阴影提亮器，炫目而奇异的补光
在你摇晃一个满载的竹篮时发生。
这个物件的轻似乎减少着
里面被拎起物品的重。

刹那间你的双手释然，
被抛下，失落，被穿过。
然后出乎意料地反弹——
向下，重返，确认你。

我想起这个盛满栗子的竹篮，
实实在在的收获，摩擦
与光亮，富足且饱满，
金黄的肚囊像一个钱袋。

而我多希望它们被画出，呈现
颜料穿透表面的洞见，呈现

[①] 这首诗讲述了画家爱德华·马圭尔（Edward Maguire，1932-
1986）为诗人画像的故事。一篮栗子是画家用来补光的物品，但
最终没有被画入肖像中。该肖像现藏于北爱尔兰国家博物馆。

超越感官范围之外的绝望，
尤其是那被挫败的触觉。

自从一九七三年秋天
爱德华·马圭尔访问我们家，
一篮栗子就在我们之间发光，
他画了我，没有画它——

尽管他原以为可能用它
作为光的诱饵或者宝匣
贮藏他在我鞋尖捕捉的光。
但它不曾在画里，现在也不。

往日重现，尤其对于他。
在油彩和笔触里我们被认证。
竹篮发光，板栗的狐火闪亮，
他从中穿过，释然，失落。

教士帽

和高卢一样，教士帽被分成
三部分：三边折起的黑斜纹布，
规整如船①的平顶帽，每条斜边和边缘
都线条整齐、鲜明而坚决。

里面是压褶的绸缎；也很重
但还饰有一个毛茸茸的流苏，
我手指的背面记得清楚，
并在教士额前留下一道红印。

我的手从无论哪位主持仪式的教士
手中接过它，一种轻浅
繁琐的运动，向上向外再向内
"以圣父、圣子和圣灵的

名义……"我把它放在台阶上，

---

① 原文是"shipshape"，意思是"井井有条的，整齐的"，原指
由于船内空间有限，船员必须把物品摆放整齐。但从字面上
看，该词也有"船形"的隐含暗示，呼应教士帽的形状，且本
诗第七、八两节就直接提到船的意象。

它好像固定在那里，甚至半抗拒着
弥撒仪式所有匆忙的流程——
饮尽的圣杯和擦净的嘴唇。

第一次见到它，我听见一声大喊
如格列柯[①]笔下的苦行僧现前
宣讲地狱之火，恐龙般狂暴，
斧头在布道坛里肆意挥舞。

庇护所。大理石。跪垫。天职。
有些被压扁了，有些洁净高耸。
古老如展厅里的金戈铁甲
让我和同代人闻风丧胆。

现在我把它倒过来，它成了一条船——
一条纸船，或那条随风飘进
《炼狱篇》开头的小船
当诗歌抬起眼帘，清清嗓子。

或者那条青铜时代的小船
船桨是细针，精工的金箔脆弱
如孵化后余下的半个完好蛋壳，

---

① 埃尔·格列柯（El Greco，1541–1614），西班牙画家。

超凡脱俗的精美意象。

但最后它也像马修·洛里斯①
绘画《探访病患》里的那个，
场景在户外的河上，整体
凝重，悲怆，爱尔兰式的维多利亚风。

然而，画中，教士阁下也戴着帽子。
坚定，亲和，危难时刻被爱戴的人，
端坐倾听每一次长桨的沉浮，
为他高尚的人生难过并恪尽职守。

---

① 马修·詹姆斯·洛里斯（Matthew James Lawless，1837-
1864），爱尔兰画家。代表作《探访病患》（*A Sick Call*）现藏于
爱尔兰国家美术馆。

长凳床

遗赠，等待，终于到位并永久在此。
床体扣合，重如马车，涂着粗俗的棕色。
教堂长椅那么窄，垃圾桶那么深，方正坚固如藏经箱。

如果我躺进去，我就困在风干的松木里，
干燥如墓葬船上没有点燃的甲板。
我的大小合适，我的耳朵被遮掩。

但我听见一阵古老沉郁的潮水冲刷床头板：
无动于衷的哦哦与哦嚯，阿尔斯特
入眠时分的悠长颂歌，不甘，不败，

新教，天主教，圣经，念珠，
月光下山墙边的长谈，炉火边的靴子，
凌晨在甜美的钟声里逝去，接着是

屋瓦上的鸡鸣。
          而如今这是一份"遗产"——
端正，简朴，坚定不移，
来自久远以前，还将永远流传

一次一次又一次，载着

舌榫结构无言的美德

和不可动摇的重量。但要征服那重量，

想象许多长凳床从天而降

仿佛对人类的荒诞报复，

然后从这无害的攻击学会：无论被给予什么

永远能被重新想象，不管它碰巧

多么稳固，厚床板，笨船体，

不合时宜。你自由得像那守望者，

迷雾之上有远见的说笑者，

宣称当他从高处下来时

真实的船已从他下面被偷走。

书 包

纪念约翰·休伊特 ①

我的手工缝制的皮革书包。四十年了。
诗人，当时你处在人生的中途，
我背着它，半包都是蓝格便笺本，
看到课堂表格，展示豌豆，

墙上地图中的航路如喷泉
描述着横跨北海峡的弧线……
在我上学路上的中途，
是牛眼菊和野蒲公英。

艺不压身！书包很轻，
磨损、柔软且永远无法清空
如校园巡回魔术师的帽子。
所以拿上它，词语的宝库和馈赠，

当你体面地远走并蓦然回首
像第一天早上离开父母的孩子。

———————————

① 约翰·休伊特（John Hewitt，1907—1987）爱尔兰诗人、
学者。一九四七年，休伊特四十岁、希尼八岁，开始上小学。

重访格兰摩尔

1. 拼字游戏

纪念汤姆·德莱尼，考古学家

光石板。井水。冬日傍晚的寒冷。
我们的背也许永远不会暖但我们的脸
因明亮的炉火和热威士忌而灼烧。
即使那时已似曾相识，一种古老的
合理，一半想象或被预告，
如青枝哔哔迸发火花又燃成灰烬，
而无论那里如何骚动都无法触及我们，
炉火的光，紧闭的窗，石板与石墙。

年复一年，我们玩拼字游戏：爱
被视为理所当然，像其他任何
偶然并符合规则的字一样。
那么，"scrabble"①。不及物。
意思是去抓摸或翻找某种硬东西。
正是他听到的。我们叮叮当当的刮擦工具。

---

① 拼字游戏。也指"抓"。

2. 婴儿床

镰刀斧头和修枝剪，大门的尖叫，
孩子们过去总在门上摇荡，
拨火棒，煤斗，火钳，砂耙——
昔日的活动重新开始，
始于不同方式。我们独处，
多年后在同样的安乐之乡，
不再是租客，而是完全拥有
一幢空房屋和我们之间留下的一切。

一定不仅仅是留念，尽管
婴儿床又复归原位，凯瑟琳①
曾在黎明的床上醒来，咕咕咕
回答马路对面农舍的鸡鸣——
那也是我自己睡过的婴儿床
那时我全部的世界就是咿咿喔喔的农舍。

_____

① 希尼的女儿。

3. 场景切换

在一位朋友把他的名字刻在桦树上
仅仅几天后，我们的孩子就剥掉了树皮——
我第一次真的对他们发脾气。
我在屋子里挥舞手臂像一个狂怒的人，
现在看来也许过分了，尽管
当时这件事的确把我激怒；
它让我想起那些兄弟结盟的场景，
两个印第安勇士割腕交臂作为标志。

曾像暴露的骨头那样闪光的地方现已痊愈。
树皮变肿了并鼓起一道疤痕——
如一幕指认场景中的主人公，
老保姆看到旧伤疤，皱紧眉头
（对这一切意味着什么感到震惊）
而泪水又震惊了战争归来的老兵。

4. 一九七三年

屋顶的波纹铁咆哮如雷电，

三月来临；当一年变暖

病人和根茎都从底下出来，

我在天窗后继续冬眠，

凝望山丘上摇撼的树枝，

隔绝，像一个生病的农民

无感于时节的更迭变换，

陷入烟云和烟灰的霾雾。

接着大斋节来临，依然像雄狮，

肌腱发达并且疯狂自律，

坚定的斋戒意志肆虐全身；

而我用尼古丁的味道挑衅它，

点燃一根根香烟，兴奋，

复苏，在书房的深深洞穴。

5. 涤罪十四行

破门而入：从一开始，
词语带给我的兴奋远多于恐惧——
那时也是，当我进入自己的
假面舞会成为一个有产者。
即使那时，我的第一冲动绝不是
双重闩门或紧锁大门；
量身定制的百叶窗和拉下的帷帘
似乎过于自我保护和紧张。

但是再进来时，我吓到自己，
我是最初的入侵者，受到指示
把旧床架锯断，因为楼梯
太窄无法通过。这是坏举动，
结局如此希腊，如此危险，
唯有纯净的言行保护家园。

6. 床头读物

整个地方更加敞亮。当我们醒来

夏日的参天大树在眼前拂动

小小的常青藤嫩枝爬进房屋

除非有人训练它们出去——犹如记忆

长久以来被你训练有素，偶尔露出容颜

同时保持距离。白嘴巴的沮丧

像一条海豚游出它的影子，

带着潮湿、无法读懂、毫无掩饰的眼睛。

我游在荷马中。第二十三卷。①

奥德修斯和珀涅罗珀终于

一起醒来。其中一根床柱

是一棵古老的橄榄树的活树干

也是他们的秘密。我们的，可能是常青藤，

常青，战栗，未曾说出。

---

① 指《奥德赛》第二十三卷。

7. 天 窗

你支持安装天窗。^① 我反对
割开沧桑的油松木板的舌榫
结构。我喜欢它又低又封闭，
引起幽闭恐惧、在屋顶做巢的
效果。我喜欢干燥的感觉，
古老的天花板像完美的箱子盖。
在那下面，就是笼舍和孵化处。
青石瓦保暖如同午夜的茅屋顶。

但是当石瓦被取下，盛大的
天空进来，让惊奇保持敞开。
连续数日我觉得自己就像那间
屋子里的房客，那个瘫痪的人
从屋顶被放下来，他的罪被宽恕，
他的病被治愈，他拿起褥子走了。

———————

① 此处的"你"指希尼的妻子。她坚持在阁楼开一扇天窗。

枕上的头

晨光。珍珠母的
夏天早早到来。被刺破的胭脂红，
被冲刷的牛奶蓝。

要成为第一个路人，
与地面薄雾和山鸡一同起床。
要更年长而感激，

这一次你也有些感激
那阵痛的到来——准备就绪，
头脑清晰，预知

那创伤，克服它，
心甘情愿。
（第一次时，你沮丧，穿着

剪短的白棉布袍，
更像新娘而非大地母亲
爬上护栏床，

如今从容自若

入院前还在

码头散步。)

然后晚些，我几乎晕过去，

当被轻拍的触手可及的小女婴

递到我手上；但一如既往

在两只睁大的眼睛里醒来，

那双眼被黎明照得比以往

更深更远，看遍所有那些

等待的朝晨中的最后一个

而你鼓鼓的额头是长久的沉默

不是黎明时分的鸟鸣。

皇家景色

沿着泰晤士河前往汉普顿宫
漫游那天，他们差点中暑。
她留着侍童头，脖子裸露，
他如在梦中，为她痴狂
却故意装作远隔千里，
研究船在水中的航迹。
看这些照片。她头朝一边，
穿无袖衫，一边裸肩高耸，
一边手臂松弛，像一只垂下翅膀的小鸟
惊慌躲藏。他直直望着你，
不设防，充满爱意和海誓山盟，
很久以前的年轻王太子。
下一张是都铎建筑正面的低矮红墙。
没有别的照片了，然而现在
我们就在那里如同青草和防晒油的
气息，站在那里如同他们的第六感
在他们身后和迷宫的入口，
无缘无故地心碎，但愿他们
大胆走入他们为之迷失的中心……
相反，如同影像蹒跚穿过扭曲的玻璃，

他们再次出现，如在一部颗粒面的

黑白旧新闻片，片中他们的游船

在聚光灯下返回，渡过下沉的桥，

唯有他们顺流而下毫发无伤，

泥泞的两岸之间伤者整夜咆哮

朝着没有火焰的爆炸和没有回声的炮火——

在这一切之中不祥地呈现着

他们如何在历史中自由通行，

像丝绸裙摆拂过麻风病人，

或一对皇室宠儿的安全通行证，

畅通无阻，令人嫉妒，精神抖擞，

所以就让他们保留自己的账目

并在必要时分做出解释。

因为，尽管公允地说，他们的命运

公平合理，人们依然有权抗辩

他们被授予的每项权利和头衔

（而且在法庭里，无害本身

从未得到赞同或被宣告无罪。）

回　顾

一

整个地带显然漂浮起来：
每条路都桥连着水或在水边，
陆地成了岛屿，田渠成为护城河。

香蒲驻守湖岸：我必须
赤脚涉过海绵似的冰冷沼泽
（柔软的湖底，沼泽水渗透

野草的网络）去接近那些
常年反常并干燥的事物，
比如扎根淤泥的白垩或丝绒。

万物流入水彩。
天际线满到边缘
仿佛大地就要溢出来，

仿佛我们游移于洪水最初的暗涌，
记住，在某个地方，秘密井泉的
涌动和流淌使道路成为江河。

二

另一条他们似乎一直重复的旅行线路

是前往格伦谢恩山口——他的"泪水之路"①,

他每次都会这么说,并指出他去寄宿学校

上学的路上第一次看到的小溪。

然后他会援引约翰·戴维斯爵士②

讲述一六〇八年他与奇切斯特一起

从邓甘嫩到那里的旅程报告:

"野蛮的居民对国王代理人

惊诧的程度就像维吉尔笔下的鬼魂

见到埃涅阿斯活着下到地狱。"

他们喜欢身后开阔的山谷,

仿佛一个斜倚世界的梯子,

---

① "泪水之路"(Trail of Tears): 一八三八至一八三九年,美国
总统安德鲁·杰克逊实施清除印第安原住民的政策。切罗基族
原住民被迫离开密西西比河以东的土地,迁至今天的俄克拉荷
马州。切罗基人将这场迁徙称为"泪水之路"。

② 约翰·戴维斯爵士(Sir John Davis, 1569-1626),英国诗
人,议员,后成为爱尔兰首席检察官,支持英国政府在阿尔斯
特地区建立种植园。下文提到的奇切斯特(Arthur Chichester,
1563-1625)是英国派到爱尔兰的"巡抚",后升级为总督,种
植园事件中的主要人物,占有爱尔兰人的土地,分给非天主教
的苏格兰人所有。包括下文提到的邓甘嫩(Dungannon)地区。

他们爬上去但也可能掉落

坠入他们扛在肩上的

全部的天空与虚无。

      熟悉的道路

上升、上升，这是恋爱之地，

他们的车上天堂，人人都在

暮色里停车假寐，而云朵在

光亮的屋顶和沉睡的窗帘深处

如烟移动。

      看，他们在那儿，

迷途在应有尽有的山堡，

那里，空气是另一种呼吸而青草如一声低语，

他们感到兴奋但依然有所克制：

年轻的夫妻，惯于在门内做合法的事情，

不适合这份诱人的甜蜜。

没有在灯芯草里筑巢，没有压碎石楠的铃铛，

也没有品尝山溪的爱饮。

所以当他们返回，他们带回野蛮住民

斋戒的眼睛，在山巅下方不远处

沉默停车，在那里，陡坡

延宕如一座露台，然后仿佛陡然

降至男爵领地和百户区。
黄昏是清澈见底的水坝。
场景历历在目，游览持续，
他们凝望远方，直到他松开
刹车，快速地自由滑行
然后挂挡，伴着一如既往的
高音旋律及其渐渐的消隐。

营 救

在睡眠的漂流中我来到你身边
你被埋在齐腰的雪中。
你伸出手臂：我苏醒
像一场雪融之梦的水。

轮中轮 ①

一

我第一次真正抓住什么

是我学习踩单车的时候，

（用手）踩一辆倒立的单车，

把后轮转得超乎寻常地快。

我爱那辐条消失的情景，

爱车轴与车圈之间的空间

发出透明的嗡鸣。如果你扔

一个土豆进去，旋转的气流

会甩你一脸土豆泥的细雨；

如果你用稻草碰它，稻草粉碎。

脚蹬起初明显地抗拒你

然后开始推动你的手向前

进入新的冲力——所有那一切进入我

像自由力量的入口，仿佛信仰

抓起并旋转信仰的对象

在一个与企盼相接的轨道上。

---

① 原文是 "wheels within wheels"，形容错综复杂的情况，通常
受到神秘力量的影响。

二

但是永远没个够。不管怎样，

有谁曾在既定事实中看到局限？

我们家后面的田野里有一口井

（我们叫它"井"。它更像一个坑

里面有水，一边是小小的山楂树，

另一边是泥泞、堆满粪便的

渗流，全都被牛群踩过）。

我也爱那井。我爱那浑浊的气味，

那污水坑里的生物闻起来像陈旧的链条油。

接下来，我把单车带到那里。

我让车座和车把倒立在

柔软的坑底，我让轮胎

触到水面，然后转动脚蹬

直到它像磨坊的水车轮溅起水花

（但这是反过来的①且如摆动马尾）

令人振奋、沉浸水中的后轮

在我眼前旋起泥泞的蕾丝，

---

① "反过来"指的是，磨坊水车是水力驱动，诗中的情景是反过来的，即人转动车轮、驱动水。

让我沐浴于重生的泥雨。

连续数周我制作淤泥的光环。

然后车轴堵塞，车圈生锈，链条折断。

三

那以后再没有什么能与之相比

直到，在一个环形马戏场，在击鼓声和聚光灯里，

女牛仔们旋转入场，个个都纯洁无瑕

在静止的绳索中心。

永动。皮鲁埃特单脚旋转。

杂技演员。吟游诗人。环绕玫瑰①。保留！

---

① 原文为 Ring-a-rosies，是英国十八世纪经典童谣，亦演变为边唱边跳的游戏。孩子们手拉手围成一圈跳舞，唱起"绕啊绕啊绕玫瑰"，唱到"我们都倒下"时，最后倒下的孩子就要被罚站到中央，成为"玫瑰"，被大家围绕。据说这首童谣与十七世纪的"黑死病"有关。

雨　声

纪念理查德·艾尔曼[1]

一

整晚泛滥的雨打在阳台
木板上。我凝神却不多想
雨水漫长的苦工，然后醒来，
在淌水的屋檐和天光中，自言自语
那些说给逝者的无足轻重的套话。
比如人们会想念他或者节哀顺变。

二

也许是佩列杰尔金诺那些被水浸透、
杂草丛生的花园：他陷入遐想，
当他从暮冬的昏暗向外凝望，
柑橘和清澈的伏特加点亮暮色，
帕斯捷尔纳克，宽容而严峻，

---

① 理查德·艾尔曼（Richard Ellmann，1918–1987），杰出的美
国学者，牛津大学教授，为许多爱尔兰作家立传，如乔伊斯、
叶芝、王尔德等。

从容不迫地为自己作答。

"我感觉欠了一大笔债，"

他说（据记载）。"那么多年

只写抒情诗、只做翻译。

我感到有义务……时间飞逝。

尽管它①还有很多缺点，它的价值胜过

那些早期作品……更丰富，更人性。"

也有可能是雅典大街上的

融雪和水洼，威廉·阿尔弗莱德②站在

湿漉漉的门阶上，想起他六十岁

就过世的朋友。"《夏潮》之后

本该有一种深化，你知道，

某种更充实的东西……啊好吧，再道晚安。"

三

屋檐是夏日倾盆大雨的

水帘和连击：你被泡在好运里，

我听见它们说，泡在，泡在，泡在好运里。

---

① 指的是小说《日瓦戈医生》。

② 威廉·阿尔弗莱德（William Alfred，1922-1999），哈佛大学
中世纪文学研究者、戏剧家，住在哈佛附近的雅典大街。

也听见洪水，从下方聚集，

等待并预示，像一部杰作

或一个溢出自身的盛名。

养 子

"那由水养育的深沉的绿"

在学校我爱一幅画中深沉的绿——
地平线上架起风车的长臂与风帆。
磨坊宁静的轮廓。它们恰当的位置
映在运河中甚至更恰当了。
我不记得从何时起就知道
一片黄昏时分泥泞泛滥的[①]
土地的内在水力学。
我淤塞的希望。我心灵的低地。

存在的深沉。而诗歌
迟缓于日常事物的无风带。
我等着，直到快五十岁
才相信奇迹。像白铁匠用铁罐
做的树钟。这么久天空才明朗，
时光辉耀，心轻亮。

---

① 诗中的"黄昏"（dailigone）和"泥泞"（glar，glit）为爱尔兰语单词。

第二部分

方　阵

1. 灵　光

i

游移的光辉。冬日的光
在门廊里，而门前石阶上
一个乞丐在剪影中战栗。

于是，或可进行特别审判：
裸壁残垣和积雨的冰冷壁炉——
明亮的积水中，浮云的生命无魂地游荡。

受命完成这场旅行后，又怎样？
没有壮景，没有未知。
从遥远处遥望，孑然一身。

也没有什么特别的，
不过是旧真相破晓：没有下一局。
空旷无顶。焕发新知的风。

ii

重建屋顶。加固。掘壕防御。
用铁罐喝水。体会厨房的冰凉，
门锁，门闩，钳子，炉栅。

触摸横梁，打铁入墙，
悬一根线以核实
门梁、顶石与炉膛是否垂直。

重新安置门槛的基石。
用嵌入山墙的窗格测定方阵。
在无人注意的楼层建你的书房。

按捺每一个冲动如按下螺栓，稳固
感觉的堡垒。不要波及
语言。不要在语言中波动。

iii

方阵？在弹珠游戏中，方阵
指的是你弹出弹珠前被许可的
所有对角、瞄准、虚击、眯眼，

所有拇指的弯曲、绷紧和压力，
试探与收回，重新盘察，
所有你双臂对于盲目的确定性

抱有希望的方式，它们在那
孤注一掷后将依然持续。
百万之百万的精确发生

在你肌肉的伸展和三孔
一线的空间之间。
你从世界的天窗向外觑探。

iv

人海之下，罗马剧场的
人群可以听到另一种
更加强大的海潮滚滚而来。

就像在听得到大海的地方将海螺
托向耳边时听到的平静讯息：
现场正在说出的台词抵达

回荡在骨灰瓮的围壁。
尘封的空气滚落，滔滔不绝的
古典拗口之词扩音又消逝。

上方是多么空灵又多么坚实，
暴露于世，飘然，变幻，
出神，如潮水或音乐中的休止。

v

玩弹珠的人在水泥未干的水泥路上
用拇指按出的三个弹孔依然存在，
他们自己消失到澳大利亚已有

三十余载。三个音孔用来
持续演奏随心所欲的音乐。
吹响并聆听低音的伴奏，

那是你平缓的呼吸一度吹过
空瓶的声音。即兴。无拘无束
就像陈年干草在多风的树篱上

高扬纤弱的来生。陶笛般的大地。
三个潜听哨在高处被烤干的一排座位上
聆听下方双耳罐的共鸣。

vi

一次，童年的哈代来到一片
牧羊的田野，他假装死去
平躺在羊群娇小的小腿间。

在羊儿轻嗅、啼叫的芳草地，
他试验着无限。
他冰凉的小额头像一面铁砧等待

天空让它唱响他哑默生命的
完美音高，他在熙攘的羊毛中
引起的骚动是最初的

涟漪，并将由此向外漫漾
八十载，它最后一道圈环依然
是他心里那同一道涟漪。

vii

（我记错了。弗洛伦斯·艾米莉①说，

哈代爬过一片母羊的牧场，

为了与羊群面面相视，

它们无知的眼神和容易恐慌的

天性让他不再那么孤独，

让预料之中的悲伤在他身上

短暂驻留，了然于心并确定无疑。

接着，羊群的惊慌继续漫涌

漫入他功成名就的晚年聚会

他在其中见到的眨眼、私语和跑题，

那时他想象自己是一个幽灵

并以那全新的视角周旋其中。）

---

① 哈代的第二任妻子。

年鉴上说，当克隆马克诺伊斯①的僧侣

在礼拜堂内集体祈祷时

一艘船出现在他们上空。

船后的锚缓慢拖动，那么深，

以至于钩住了圣坛的围栏

然后，当摇晃的巨船终于停稳，

一名船员抓住绳索爬下来

奋力想要释放船身。但没用。

"此人无法忍受我们这里的生活，会淹死的。"

住持说，"除非我们帮他。"所以

他们照做，获释的船启航，船员登返，

离开他所见证的奇迹。

---

① 克隆马克诺伊斯修道院，建立于公元五四四年，位于爱尔兰
奥法利郡。

ix

从前，一只小船不摇不晃

栖息在高高的草丛，那是

星期天下午，一九四一或一九四二年。

内伊湖上，牛群拥挤躁动的

绿树篱旁，热浪里弥漫着

花呢衣裙和花呢衣袖的芬芳，

我就在那裙袖的怀抱。我依稀记得

脚跟在木板上轻快击出的尖锐木音，

偎依在臂弯里的我如一个秘密

此刻公开，如彼时睁开的天堂之眼

照在三姐妹上方，她们稳坐小船谈天，

船底的大地依然在沉陷，沉陷。

x

青草和桦树苗垂悬在
采石场表层。你在岩顶注视
所有满载的光明行于

水上、对岸或者绚丽横穿
矿床上清澈、深邃而危险的
孔洞中的水域。终极的

深可见底，终极的
负隅顽抗：你能否调和
那里兼具的空灵与厚重？

那如此混沌而轻盈的构造，
你和它相同，还是相反？
闭上眼睛，仰望并直面音乐①。

---

① 原文 "face the music" 有 "毅然直面困难或不好后果" 之意。
《布里吉德之环》一诗第三节中也有此表达。

xi

将玻璃屋顶装在手球球场
那里跃起的球曾划出无情的角度
界内或出界，或精准发出

那个无法应答的死球……
唯有他，我们行走的风信鸡，
我们画架前警觉的眼睛，有权

将那自由的迷宫作为画室，
将外面的光引进并控制这空间
耍弄花招让偶然变成精确

并让雨更加雨，当它被风
吹过水泥地的网格和纹理。
他以臂距绘制世界，竖起拇指。

那么灵光？其另一重含义

超越平常意义上的减轻

或照亮，等等，指的是：

一个非凡的瞬间，灵魂

在临死前焕发出纯喜之光——

我们心中的义贼①听守希望！

所以，把他画在基督右边，在海岬上

环顾苍茫，饱受肉体折磨的他

仿佛无法通过移译进入极乐

无法通过脑后的钉孔抵达

前额月轮怀有的痛切渴望：

今日你将与我同在乐园。

---

① 根据《新约·路加福音》，耶稣被钉上十字架时，有两个盗贼
陪同，其中一个为"义贼"，他希望耶稣抵达天国时能想起他。

2. 场 景

xiii

榛树的秘密行动。水滴淌在涵洞。

活跃的灯塔之光映在门阶的石板上，

在海面上，在沉寂的屋顶和山墙。

白石灰的向阳处。树篱热得像烟囱。

椅子们四脚着地。沥水架牢固负重。

灶台和板岩的化石之诗。

欲望在它自己的城壕里，安闲打盹——

像正午礁石上吃饱的鸬鹚，

被流放，与炫烈的闪光和鸣。

再次进入这里，作为孤寂的成人，

涉过沉寂者，以及你感到的那个

确定的在场——那个初来时曾退缩的人。

一天下午，我是金叶上的六翼天使。

我站在铁轨枕木上聆听云雀、

草蜢、布谷、犬吠、教练机

掠过、转向并远去的轰鸣。

热浪徘徊在纯洁无瑕的铁轨

和闪闪发光的齿轮。两边，

雏菊伫立如贞女，灼热的石子

被三叶草缠绕，沾染着机油。

空气弥漫，等候通行，保持平衡，

没有什么盛行。凡要发生的

都见证着自身已然发生

在以应许和间隙为标志的时间里。

xv

也用黄金打造这一幕吧，浮雕，
以便贪婪的眼睛都无法穷尽：
马厩的草，伦勃朗式的微光与明亮

我父亲俯身在装满盐的茶箱前，
左手攥紧拳头把防风油灯
举在眼前，右手摸索着

不流血的、肉色鲜明的培根，
自制的火腿，拿到灯下
思索片刻又放了回去。

那晚我拥有埃及成堆的谷物。
我观察哨兵的火炬照耀库存。
我站在门内，隐身而被照亮。

xvi

老鼠药是血布丁的颜色，

被泼撒时发出幽幽磷火：

刀口下火花四射的腐臭光芒

让一切复活——就像听到谋杀新闻

或瞥见路边停放的汽车里

有一对恋人，或斗牛士遇难的故事。

即使是缪斯歌唱阿喀琉斯的愤怒

也不会为世界带来更多危险。

一切尽在新鲜的老鼠药里，

发霉的干面包皮上电光闪闪。

在冬日的夜晚我喜欢它的臭味和风险。

被风吹落的果实冻结在茅屋顶上。

xvii

鳗鱼皮有什么好处？鳗鱼

本身又是什么？从水中抽出的

水之肋骨，一个 L，生自

那些暗涌、旋涡和石瓦蓝的深海，

剥皮时才被重新发现。

手腕绑上鳗鱼皮，能量

注入那条手臂，一个水轮

在你肩膀旋转，水槽倾注，

让你的肘部眩晕。

你的手感到无拘无束而且振奋

如同淤泥里蠕动的脑袋和尾巴

亚里士多德认为那是所有鳗鱼的起源。

xviii

像一个说话粗鲁的麻绳之神开始发情，

那个编麻绳的人重重地走来，夸赞新绳

说它多么粗，或者多么长，多结实，

你怎么把它握在自己手中

感受它。他完美而紧实的绳子

围着他绕了一个圈：缰绳、

腹带、笼头的机制。然后绳索滑落——

即使那时，我的身高刚到农民的膝盖，

我已知道那编麻绳的人正以一种他们

终将背离的自由不羁造成威胁；也知道

他的无力，一旦集市山变得空荡，

他不得不冲出重围，开始装货。

xix

记忆作为一幢楼或一座城，

灯火通明，布局合理，充满

活画场景①和盛装模特——

披紫色斗篷的雕像，或涂成红色的，

戴着冠冕的，涂着泥或血的：

以便心灵的目光能运用

固定的联想萦绕自身并学会

按照意味深长的顺序阅读自心，

古老的课本建议我们

用意象的代码审慎地连起

熟悉的地点。你知道每一个

场景的征兆，你眨眼且专注。

---

① 活画场景（tableaux vivants），活人扮演的静止场景，起源于
中世纪的欧洲，多用来表演圣经故事。

xx

在红场，克里姆林宫的砖墙

看起来没有威胁，在规模上，恰好适合人们

在下面、里面或外面规矩行动。

正面巨大的空地令人目眩。

我环顾起伏铺展的卵石

仿佛我梦里熠熠发光的石头

梦中我飞在老马路上空，所有气流

在我的脖子和胸骨下方扇动。

（云游者，斯大林是这样称呼帕斯捷尔纳克的吗？[①]）

恐怖的历史和被保护的欢乐！

一九四〇年代公路上的马粪炸药。

新闻片里的爆炸袭击，无害如硝烟。

[①] 斯大林曾这样说起捷尔纳克："让他安歇吧，他是个云游者。"

xxi

有且仅有一次我开了枪——

一把点22^①。朝着六十码以外

一块钉在树上的四方手帕。

这让我兴奋——子弹之歌

在我指尖不费吹灰之力，

靶子唯一的小小悸动，

对"步枪"有了全新而鲜活的理解。

然后一如从前我再一次

看到灵魂像一块白布被夺走

穿过黑暗的星系并感到那次射击

是对永恒生命犯下的罪过——

另一个词组在新的光芒里扩展。

---

① 一种口径 0.22 英寸的枪械。

xxii

灵魂居于何处？内部还是外部，

记忆中的事物，造物，未造物？

哪个在先，海鸟的啼鸣还是当它

在黎明的寒冷中啼鸣时被想象的灵魂？

它最后栖归何处？古老石塔上方

寒鸦巢中沾着粪便的枯枝？

还是俯视花坛的大理石半身像？

完结的身形在多大程度上可栖？

以及如何居于那多风的光亮？

保持音或持续的诗行有什么用

若不能接受批评、打消疑虑？

（给 W.B.① 的鬼魂的一组提问。）

---

① 指叶芝。

xxiii

乘坐巴士前往萨迦的国度

伊文·马林诺夫斯基[1]写了一首诗

关于一艘从废弃的捕鲸站

离开口岸的核潜艇。

我记得这首诗令人激动，

却想不起一个字。当时我想要的

是一首讲述极致之夜的诗：

十三世纪，怪异的午夜太阳

落在斯诺里·斯特鲁森[2]眼前

当时他正在外面泡温泉

坐享挤奶时间之后的宁静，

沐浴并安住在他心灵的宫殿。

---

① 伊文·马林诺夫斯基（Ivan Malinowski，1926–1989），丹麦
诗人、政治评论家。
② 斯诺里·斯特鲁森（Snorri Sturluson，1179–1241），冰岛历
史学家、诗人、政治家。

荒凉海港的宁静。每一粒石子
都在水下澄清并安眠，
海港墙是一堵沉默的堡垒。

充实。微茫。汹涌的大西洋，
码头几乎不为所动，只有海浪
冲击船板时发出轻微的声响。

完美的视野：鸟蛤的宣礼塔
被下放到那里，连同绿而滑的瓶玻璃、
碎螺壳和一朵砂岩的红蕾。

众所周知，天空与海洋互为
前身。两者同时并列于
遍在，平衡，充盈。

3. 穿 越

黎明启程向南，全速出发

穿过高高的石墙区，岩石依然冰冷，

雨水在前方各处闪烁，

我转弯，遇见一只一动不动的狐狸，

在路中央与它面面相觑。

我浑身激动，只见它低头转身

一场匀速奔跑的橘色逃离。

哦，精致的头、传说中的茸尾和受惊的眼睛，

与我的蓝色大众和晨光交相辉映！

就让新生到来，通过水，通过渴望，

通过诊室地板上的匍匐倒行：

我必须穿越回去，通过那受惊的虹膜。

xxvi

年复一年，只能从后面接近

那些车厢敞开、帆布顶篷的卡车，

里面坐满拥挤而忠诚的士兵。

他们手握枪管，目光涣散，

从烫人的金属向外凝望如在梦中。

沉默，不为时间所动，在挡风玻璃后

保持均等的距离，被公路

幻影般的逆流载向前方，

依然要完成此时此地的任务。

所以不要引起注意，驾驶并凝神于

逃逸的空间，如同灵魂在地狱

沾满稻草的坚冰上加速熔毁。

xxvii

万物流动。即使一个结实的男人，

他自己和他生意的顶梁柱，

黄靴子、桦木杖、软毡帽，

也会脚底生翅健步如飞

成为赶集日、石柱、公路和十字路口的神，

旅人守护者和灵魂指引者。

"在船上找一个拿桦杖的男人，"

我父亲告诉他即将前往伦敦的

妹妹，"整晚待在他附近，

你会平安无事。"流动，流动

灵魂的旅行，伴着灵魂向导

和神秘的拿手杖的生意人！

xxviii

冰就像玻璃瓶。我们排起队

渴望再进入那个长滑梯，

是我们使它臻于完美，一次又一次

奔跑、就绪然后释放

进入一种极致，它自身的回报：

告别稳健的步履，运动场

超出我们一如既往的自控。

那正在进行的继续进行，从抓住到放手，

黑暗坚冰中的狭窄银河，

前冲、自由驰骋然后返回——

像一个光的圆环自相追逐

我们自知已然安渡并将继续航行。

xxix

弹簧锁唐突的咔哒响。
冰冷传到拇指。跷跷板似的
起落与天真无邪的噪音。

一种约束与释放的音乐
这一代人没有听过，但只要
重新触碰就能唤起或平息它。

一旦弹簧锁发声，屋顶
就复原如初，门槛致命，
强大的惩罚如不祥之兆。

你的脚步已被听出，那么
微微欠身，举起右手，
让冲动与意愿合一，请进。

xxx

在圣布里吉德节，穿过她用草绳
编的环就可以迈入新生：
男人的正确做法是先迈右腿，

然后右臂和右肩，头，然后左
肩、左臂和左腿。女人把它从头顶
套在身上然后再迈出去。

他们通过这些动作进入的开阔
变得更加开放，圈环从世界滑落，
他们能感到头顶上空

二月的空气依然柔和，并想象
松垂的绳索磨损闪耀像风吹扬谷粒
或自由无阻的黄雀飞过耕地。

xxxi

没有林荫道也没有林荫。

大约四分之一英里，县道

直穿北安特里姆的沼泽，

参天的古杉列队两边。

苏格兰冷杉。书法体的禾束

在盛行风中蓬蓬簇簇。

你驶入树木制成的意义。

或者准确地说并非树。而是一种

在树间树下畅行无阻的感觉，

浮光掠影。汽车从雪泥鸿爪的

生活中消失。扑扇的项背

敏感于百万分之一的颤动。

xxxii

流水从不让人失望。

跨过水面总会促生什么。

踏脚石是灵魂的驿站。

柳条路①是一条小径，有人称为堤道，

路面高出潮湿的沼泽，

或连接起旧渠与小溪。

说起这些让我安心。而且

只要提到堤道或浅滩

我父亲的鬼魂必然显现

在面朝日落的路上，打量铁锹和衣裳

那是割泥炭的人们收拾好的，或者灵魂丢掉的

在它们跨越那根横跨小溪的圆木之前。

---

① 原文是 "kesh"，爱尔兰方言，指的是用柳条编织，再铺上泥土和石子的小路，用来跨过沼泽或湿地。

xxxiii

暂且现实片刻。回忆

外出散步时走在他死后

被清空的地方，然后转身离去。

那天早上，石瓦更硬，窗更冷，

窗格上的雨滴更凄凉，青草

更无遮蔽地面向天空，更加飘摇，

或看似如此。他设计的房子

"朴素，宽大，端正，普通，你知道，"

一种缜密与准确的范式，

反对浮夸，致敬界限，

比以往更坚守它自身的理念，

像为 X 射线穿透的身体冲印的 X 光片。

xxxiv

叶芝说，对于那些见过幽灵的人，人的皮肤

此后很长一段时间都显得格外粗糙。

我在车厢过道里见到的那张脸

却完全不是这样：我乘巴士

从旧金山机场前往伯克利，

车上还有另一名乘客，他在

珍宝岛军事基地下车

在湾区大桥的中途。他要去越南，

他很可能是从刚死的那些人中回来的。

不惊不惧但依然失望，

不得不再次承受他农家少年的自我，

他剃须的伤痕，他彼世的额头。

xxxv

剃须的伤痕。坏习惯的苍白。

星期天下午，夏日悠闲，

情侣们沿着福伊尔河漫步，

我们把一面剃须镜拿到

寄宿生宿舍顶层的窗户：

幸福山谷的恋人，后排

饥渴而静默的汽车，绝对的河

横亘在我们和那一切之间。我们把镜子

倾斜放入阳光中，确定射程，用一道

快闪的光照射我们无法拥有的事情。

光亮在他们身上随机嬉戏

如同神的盾牌或舞池地板的反光。

xxxvi

是的，我的朋友，我们也曾穿过山谷。
一次。在黑暗中。所有街灯都熄了。
当危险逼近，游行被驱散。

但丁的场景，因为一个令人
头脑清醒的比喻而更加难忘——
比如，萤火虫，警察的手电筒

聚集、闪烁并诱惑我们信任
他们不可预测的迷人之光。
我们就像成群的幽魂不得不穿越

且确实穿越，惊慌失措地来到
我们之前停放的车前，上车时
像卡戎的小船在游吟诗人身下摇晃。

4. 方　阵

xxxvii

在智者寒山的著名诗中

寒山是一处地方，也意味着

一种心境，或不同时刻的

不同心境。这些诗仿佛

一气呵成，随性，比如以下开篇：

"一向寒山坐，淹留三十年"

或者"人问寒山路，寒山路不通"——

令人嫉妒的文字，

不雕琢，诚可信。

这样谈论还不够好

但引用它至少表明

艺术的美德在知自心。

xxxviii

我们在月光下爬上朱庇特神庙，

感到峰巅之上的诱惑与极乐：

我们荣幸、来迟并深知。

然后我有感而发作出预言

针对那些恃宠而骄的冰冷石像

和所有壮志凌云的石刻诗行。

"推翻宏大形象，"（我说）

"行乞与康复的形象万岁。我们等候

净水和转经轮的回归。"

一个声音答道，"我们当然在等。

但其他人在广场咖啡厅等候，

好奇我们在哪儿。你想喝点什么？"

xxxix

当你坐在巨人堤"许愿椅"的
玄武岩王座，目光深远而冷峻，
你小小的腰背给人坚实的感觉。

像早春时节绑在枫树上的印第安小孩，
你从世界之树的坚硬里汲取力量。
如果你伸一伸手，事物会变成石头。

但你只是起满鸡皮疙瘩的皮包骨，
礁石和世界奇观不过是
凝结的熔岩，大地上的盐

被许愿椅赋予一种风味，
巨藻和臭氧刷新你的视野
超出你准备接受的范围。

xl

我当时四岁，但也许四百岁，
当我面对一块黏土地板
古老潮湿的感觉。甚至可能四千岁。

总之，就是这样。臭水洼里倒给
猫喝的牛奶，陶水罐周围布满
被溅出的水弄黑的霉。

存在的地基。身体深深服从
它全部的变化时态。一扇半门
直接敞向浩瀚的星光。

从那座土房子，我继承了
一叠独特而冰凉的记忆砝码
把我从头到脚置于万物的天平。

沙床，他们说。砾床。在我
知道河流的浅滩或河流的乐趣前
我知道那些词里蕴含渴望的矿石。

我重返的那些地方还在
但不会持久。站在齐腰的牛欧芹中，
我再度进入河流，驾驭或平息

那些构成记忆的水流，
不断积聚的万事万物
当我在黄昏时分布下方阵

站在桥头或者自我的河岸。
恐惧轻舔。甜蜜瞬间。挑逗和泼溅。
没入天空的垂柳轻抚起皱的柔波。

xlii

石楠花、柳条路和堆叠的泥炭

一个个夏天依然重现，蚂蚱及一切，

依旧但更罕见：在接近福地的田野

瘦削的人们穿着衬衫弯腰挖掘

或在黄昏独自伫立审视沼泽岸——

如今是幽灵，但依然活跃

且坚守地盘，依然明确其立场，

依然迷恋，不知道鬼魂的国度

又被向后推了多远，

云雀在田野外停留了多久，

只是对它们来说仿佛无法停下，

宛若阳光辉耀下的远山。

择一串踪迹去追踪野兔

直到足印停止，突然地，在雪里。

一行结束。积雪光滑。她去哪儿了？

当然，重返她的足迹，接着纵身

跃到几码外的一侧；干净利落；无味无迹。

她落入洞窟并开始吃雪。

也想想古代的象形文字，

"野兔与之字形"，意为"存在"，

始终保持警觉，迂回并躲闪

像我们的朋友跃出（再见）我们的视线

并终于错过一局（但他当然会请大家喝酒）：

*惊心动魄者，打落露珠者，目光长远者。*①

---

① 出自希尼翻译的中世纪英语抒情诗《野兔的名字》。

xliv

全都消失于光的世界了？也许

当我们读到这一句，纯粹的形式确实

挤满星辉熠熠的前厅。否则

他们不。光辉所超越的事物

苍白如我举起的夜晚钓线上的虫子，

永不餍足尽管永远做好准备

迎接那里的虚无——那里仅有的事物。

尽管它其实更像一条被咬钩的钓线折断，

承认全都消失的一刻，

当鱼竿的粗端失联而尖端淌水，

旋涡旋转着一枚枯叶无声漂过，

（仿佛）比水的流逝还迅捷。

对有些人来说，书里写的会成真：
他们将继续活下去，
在远方的河口。

对我们的人来说，不。他们将重新进入
干涸，那就是他们的地上天堂，
幸福地吃着泥土烘烤的司康。

对于有些人，也许是三角洲的芦苇滩，
冰冷的、脚爪光亮的海鸟永远盘旋。
对于我们的人，是烛花，

以及炉灰和灰烬的余热。
法官在一束发光的日常尘埃里
来到他们和太阳之间。

xlvi

从高山背后吹来的山风；

前方，夏末，石墙围拥的田野；

石瓦屋内，小提琴悠扬

如日落时分打水漂的扁石

或扁平大地不可挽回的尾流

依然逃逸到太空背后。

音乐可曾是上帝存在的证明？

只要承认那些不可测度之物，

那个假设就成立。

所以就让耳朵凝神，如柔光下

农舍的窗子，那超凡者一度从那里

经过，满帆驶入渴想之境。

xlvii

离开海岸或超出锚地之外

远处的可见海面

叫作远海。

它愈是空茫，审视的目光

就愈受到挑战。

而一旦你转身背对它，你的背

顿时长满眼睛如百眼巨人。

然后，你再看，远海依然

未受侵犯，但又似被清空

仿佛曾在你视线边缘操练的

发光的军队已经撤退

到天际线之后演习并重组。

xlviii

多奇怪啊，即将发生之事，一旦被觉知，

就变成预知的事；

偶然事件唯有置于已然

发生的必然事件中才显得昭彰。

第七重天或许就是

第六感邂逅的全部真相。

无论怎样，当光突然照彻我

一如它曾照彻科尔雷恩以外的公路

那里风更咸，天空更匆忙，

银锦缎在班恩河谷战栗

在油漆浮标之间的河道中途，

那天我将与被我忽略的事物同步。

穿 越

（《地狱篇》第三歌，第82-129行）

在那条朝我们驶来的小船里

有一个老人，发白如雪，

怒吼咆哮，"受苦吧，邪恶的魂灵！

哦，再也别指望看见那美妙的天空！

我前来带领你们去到彼岸，

进入永恒的黑暗，进入火与冰。

说你呢，你，活着的灵魂，将你

自己同另外这些死人分开。"

但当他见我并未站到一旁，

他说，"从另一条路，从别的港口

你将抵达不同的河岸并逾越。

承载你的是一条更轻的小船。"

然后我的向导说，"息怒，卡戎。

在那里，上帝的意愿皆可实现，

这是上天的安排；所以无须多虑。"

然后他立刻合上花白的下颌，
那片乌青色沼泽的摆渡人
眼睛周围燃烧着火轮。

但是，一听见这些残酷的话，
那些迷失的灵魂，赤裸而疲惫，
全都惊惶失色、牙齿战栗；

他们辱骂上帝和他们尘世的双亲，
辱骂人类，他们繁殖与诞生的
时间地点与温床，

然后所有人一起，痛哭流涕，
启程前往被诅咒的另一岸
那里等候每一个无惧上帝的人。

魔鬼卡戎的眼睛就像被煽动的烫煤。
他召唤他们，招呼所有人上船
并用船桨击打落在后面的。

正如一片片叶子在秋日坠落
直到唯余裸木枯枝，但见
从它那里掠去的横尸遍野，

同样，亚当的劣种在示意下
一个接一个将自己抛下河岸，
每一个都像猎鹰听从召唤。

他们就这样在褐色的水面上离开
在他们登陆到对岸之前
又一群人在此岸聚集。

"我的儿子，"谦和的老师对我说，
"所有死于上帝愤怒的人们
从四面八方聚集到这里，

他们渴望穿越这条河流
因为神圣的法官用马刺驱赶他们
以至于他们将恐惧转为企盼。

从来没有善良的灵魂经过这里，
因此，如果卡戎将你拒绝，
你应该理解他隐含的意思。"

酒精水准仪

1996

给海伦·文德勒

目 录

注释与致谢

感谢以下报刊的编者，本书中的一些诗歌曾首发于这些报刊：

《备忘录》《阿耆尼评论》《安泰》《学院绿》《学位袍》《卫报》《哈佛评论》《诚实的阿尔斯特人》《星期天独立报》《爱尔兰时报》《伦敦书评》《云母》《新共和》《新威尔士评论》《圣母评论》《牛津诗歌》《帕纳索斯》《诗歌》《诗歌与听众》《爱尔兰诗歌评论》《PN评论》《苏豪广场》《南方评论》《思考者评论》《三便士评论》《三趾鸥》《泰晤士报文学增刊》《韵文》《左页》。《在源头》《坚持下去》《磨刀石》以及《航线》的第五首曾发表在《纽约客》。

《航线》最初发表在《PN评论》第88期唐纳德·戴维七十寿辰特刊。重刊于此，悼念他一九九五年的辞世。

《解放后》最初发表在《潮起潮落》（故事线出版社，1994）；《最初的词语》改写自罗马尼亚诗人马林·索列斯库一首诗的译本，约安娜·拉塞尔-吉比特译（原载《世界上最大的蛋》，血斧书社，1987）。

雨　棒

给贝思和兰德

把雨棒倒过来，接下来发生的
是一种你从来没有听过的
音乐。在一根仙人掌茎里

骤雨，泄洪，泛滥和落潮
汹涌而过。你站在那儿像一根水
奏的管笛，你再轻轻摇晃它

渐弱贯穿它全部的音域
像檐槽挡住雨滴。而此刻又传来
焕新的树叶滴落的疏雨，

然后是青草和雏菊洒下的小雨点；
然后是闪光的细雨，近乎风的呼吸。
把雨棒再次倒过来。接下来发生的

并不因为曾发生过一次、
两次、十次、一千次而减少。
谁在乎这植物蒸腾的全部音乐

是沙砾还是干种子在仙人掌里流泻？

你仿佛一个从雨滴的耳朵

进入天堂的富人。再听一次。

致一位在爱尔兰的荷兰陶匠

给索尼娅·兰德尔

然后我进入词汇的保险库
在那里词语如浴火的陶罐
立在窑边干燥的壁龛

于是脱胎换骨，如看守见到
墓石在天空的钻光下移动
或在陶土门后瞥见牛角门。

一

我所知道的泥土很脏。河沙
是唯一洁净的东西，沉淀在
流淌、泥泞、阴冷、积水的地上。

直到我发现班恩黏土。像潮湿的天光
或黏黏的绸缎藏在毛毡与粗呢似的
腐殖层下。真正的硅藻泥

被发现于一个小小的吸孔，

灰蓝，暗光，无味，可触——
像大地古老的油膏匣，黏而凉。

那时候你正在大海里游泳
或跑出大海，发光的浮游生物，
北海边的磷光体精灵，

硅女神的圣洁贞女，
在陶瓷王国火热的中心地带
置身于青草、玻璃和灰烬下。

那时我们本可能相识，
在地下和水畔的冷辉人生。
噼啪嬉水的双生灵童。

也可能打破小小的禁忌——
玩泥巴或把秋千高高荡起，
在篱笆里玩"秘密"或"舔舌头"的游戏——

然而没有，在可怕的事件中。
相反，夜复一夜，在荷兰，
你观察轰炸机的杀戮；然后，天赐良机，

你从战争年代的火光映照中归来，

也从此后每一段幸福时日的
火石英、生铁和石灰的釉彩中归来。

而假若釉料，如你所说，使太阳陨落，
那么你的陶轮正托起大地。
荣光属于地下。燃烧的井。

荣光在于洁净的泥沙和高岭土
以及，"黑麦在废墟旁起伏"，
在于灰坑、氧化物、碎片和叶绿素。

二　解放后

1

纯粹而明媚的春。春一如既往，
清晨料峭，但当朗朗天光
旋动敞开，亘古不息的天空
是幸存者的奇迹。

在浣洗田野的明澈珠光里，
过去的事物回来；迟缓的马儿
翻犁一片休耕地，不远处，
战争隆隆逝去。

活过来并且如今拥有表达的

自由，全部身心——每一次

醒来都知道它已结束并永久地结束了，那件

几乎击垮你的事——

这一切值得，拉肢架上的五年，

反抗，顺从，而尚未出生的一代代

没有一人将如此

珍惜自由。

2

潮起潮落，它们的日常！

这颗心是什么，始终充满恐惧，

知道，正如它一定知道，春之获释，

明亮的心，恒常如潮？

无处不在，无动于衷，

是死亡发源的生命。

而抱怨是错的，哪怕最微小的怨言，

既然黑麦在废墟旁起伏。

译自荷兰诗人J.C.布鲁姆（1887-1966）

布里吉德之环

给阿黛拉[1]

我上一次写信，写于一张朴素的桌子，

在南卡罗来纳的木兰树下

木兰花落在我身上，白石灰山墙

轮廓清晰宛若白轮船的船首

在阳光下的院落平分阳光。

我享受几周以来最初的暖意

和最初的静谧。我听见嘲鸫的歌声

和杜西莫琴轻轻的叮铃

清晰悦耳地飞上天空

仿佛一群阴韵[2]向北方迁徙

在那里你面对音乐和夏日疼痛

而土地的预知在土里积聚。

现在是圣布里吉德节，第一朵雪花莲

---

① 阿黛拉（Adele Dalsimer，1939–2000），希尼的朋友，在波
士顿学院建立了爱尔兰研究项目。
② 阴韵（feminine rhyme），指一个重读音节后伴随一个或多个
非重读音节的韵。

开在威克洛，这是我正在为你编织的
布里吉德之环，如梦如幻的圈
（犹如人们编制的旧时裙撑），

拧在一起的秸秆撑起的圆圈
为了致意和治愈，春的礼仪
奇异、轻盈而传统犹如
你经由这首诗而经历的律动。

薄　荷

它看似一丛又小又脏的荨麻
在我们家山墙下疯狂生长
那是我们丢垃圾和旧瓶子的地方：
永远不够绿，不引人注意。

但是，公平地说，在我们
生活的后院，它也讲述希望与新生
仿佛某种稚嫩却顽强的东西
散布在绿色小径并蔓延开来。

剪刀的咔嚓声，星期天早上的光，
薄荷被剪下被喜爱：
我最近的事物将最先被我遗忘。
但就让所有幸存的自由自在。

就让薄荷的气味醉人且无防御，
像那边院子里被放风的囚徒。
像那些被漠视的人，我们背过身去
因为我们的漠视已令他们失望。

四十年代的沙发

我们在沙发上排排坐，跪在
彼此身后，从老大到最小，
肘部运动如活塞，因为这是一列火车

在门墙和卧室门之间
我们的速度和距离不可估量。
首先我们转轨，然后我们鸣笛，然后

有人向看不见的旅客
查票并一本正经地打孔
当一节节车厢在我们身下

越跑越快，咔嚓咔嚓，沙发腿
开始眩晕，远处厨房地板上
遥不可及的人们开始挥手。

*

鬼魂专列？葬礼贡多拉？那雕花的弧形两端，
黑色人造革和它华丽的苍凉
使这沙发仿佛获得了

浮力。它踮起足尖的脚轮，
它镶边而流畅的靠背散发
一种过时的仪式感：

当客人们忍耐它，腰板挺直，
当它保持自己遥远的距离，
当圣诞节早晨，少得可怜的玩具

出现在它上面，它还是它自己，
潜在地趋向天堂，实际上脚踏实地，
在那些令人满意或失意的事物中。

*

我们进入历史与无知，
在收音机架下。耶！
《山中骑士》的音乐响起。现在播报新闻。

权威播音员说。在他与我们之间
横亘着一道鸿沟，在那里，发音
如暴君独裁统治。一根天线

从树梢延伸下来，穿过窗框
上面的孔。当它在风中摇曳，
语言的振荡及其回声

在我们心中摇晃如水中的渔网

或远处火车抽象而孤独的曲线，

当我们进入历史与无知。

*

我们全力占据我们的座位，

已经适应这份不适。

恒心是它自身的报偿。

前方，软垫大扶手上，

有人把头伸向一旁，司机或

锅炉工，擦拭他干燥的额头

仿佛受尽酷刑。仿佛我们

是他最后的心事；我们觉察到

一条隧道出现，我们呼啸而过

像夜晚旷野里没有点灯的车厢，

我们唯一的任务是坐着，直视前方，

且行且喜并发出机车的噪音。

坚持下去

给休

那从远处走来的风笛手是你
白墙刷代替皮毛袋
在你身前摇摆，一把餐椅
倒放在肩上，你的右臂
假装把风囊夹在肘下，
你圆睁的眼睛，鼓鼓的两颊
几乎爆发出笑声，但呼吸间，
始终坚持让低音嗡鸣下去。

                    *

白墙刷。一个边缘泛白的老物件
挂在牛棚门后，等待它的时机，
直到春风招来工作桶里的石灰
以及一根搅棒去加水拌和。
那些气味让人流泪，我们吸入
一种绿色的灼烧并想到硫磺。
但真正刷墙时到处
泼溅的污水，用力铺洒在
墙上的水淋淋的灰泥，然后

逐渐变干变白，这一切就像魔法。

我们从哪里来，我们自知已经

复归的这个王国是什么？我们的影子

在墙上移动，一条柏油碎石路围绕

房子的四周闪光，一道乌黑的分界

仿佛新掘的、刺鼻的臭壕沟。

                        *

在山墙下小便，亡者会聚集。

但分别地。女人们在天黑后，

在那儿坐一会儿才睡觉，

唯有此时灵魂得以独处，

唯有此时脸庞和身体在上天

注目下获得平静。

                    脱脂乳和尿，

食品柜，家畜，聆听的卧室。

我们全都在一起，在从前，

在我们熟知但无法移译

且依然不确定是否发生过的

多风夜晚。它散发山堡泥土

和牛粪的气味。当山楂树被砍倒，

你折断手臂。我感到恐惧，

当一只怪鸟连续数日栖息在牛棚屋顶。

*

那一幕，麦克白陷入无助而绝望的

噩梦——他再次遇到那些老巫婆

并看见锅里的鬼魅幻影——

我太熟悉那场景了。壁炉，

蒸汽，哀号，烟熏的头发

遮住一边的脸颊。"到了学校，

不要接近坏男孩。听见了吗？

听见我对你说的话了吗？别忘了！"

然后搅拌棒加速搅动稀粥，

上方的蒸汽旋转，一切亲密

而恐怖的事物发出短暂的光亮，

然后逐渐暗淡、完结并消失。

*

血迹斑斑的粥状灰色物质

溅在白石灰墙上。干净的部分是

他脑袋曾在的地方，其他血迹渗入

干透的石墙，那天早晨他曾靠在

那里，和其他任何早晨一样，

兼职的预备役，拿着他的午餐盒。

一辆汽车沿城堡街缓缓驶来，停下，
穿过钻石区，再慢下来停在
他旁边，尽管不是他的顺风车。
然后他看见一张平常的脸，
毫无掩饰，还有一支枪对准他的脸。
他的右腿后钩，脚底和脚跟
抵着墙，并用右膝稳稳撑着，
所以他从未移动，只是用尽全力
支撑自己，然后倒在柏油路上，
用他丰沛的鲜血喂食阴沟。

*

我亲爱的兄弟，你有很好的耐力。
你留在事发现场，你的大拖拉机
停在钻石区，你向人们挥手，
在引擎上大喊大笑，你让出
熟悉的马路而行驶在陌生的路上。
你曾把风笛手的皮毛袋唤作白墙刷，
装扮后拉着我们快步穿过厨房，
但你不能让死者行走或校正不公。
我看到你有时也筋疲力尽，
在挤奶坊里，在两头奶牛之间
强撑着自己，直到癫痫平息，

然后又在牛粪的气味中回过神来，

思量着，这就是全部吗？仿佛

最初、现在、将来都如此？

然后揉揉眼睛看到我们牛棚

门上的旧刷子，又坚持下去。

两辆卡车

雨落在黑煤和暖湿的灰烬上。
院子里有轮胎的印痕，阿格纽的旧卡车
将全部起落架放下，阿格纽这位运煤工
正用他的贝尔法斯特口音对我母亲甜言蜜语。
她会去马拉费尔特看电影吗？
但现在下雨了，可他还有半车货物

要送到远处。这一回，我们
产煤的矿脉像黑丝绸，所以那灰烬
也将最像丝绸白。开往马拉费尔特
（经图姆桥）的车走了。那半空的卡车
连同它叠好的空煤袋打动我母亲：
穿皮围裙的运煤工的糖衣炮弹！

当然还有电影！运煤工的骄傲……
她回到屋里，取出石墨和
砂纸，这位一九四〇年代的母亲，
整天围着火炉转，用手背好歹抹去
脸上的灰烬，插上插销的卡车
加速、掉头、驶向马拉费尔特

送最后一批货。哦，马拉费尔特！
哦，梦中的红色长毛绒和城市运煤工，
当时间快进，一辆不同的卡车
咯吱咯吱进入镜头，来到大街上，载着
能让汽车站灰飞烟灭的炸弹……
那以后，我看见我母亲的幻象，

一个亡魂，坐在我常和她碰头的
马拉费尔特地板冰冷的候车室长凳上，
她的购物袋里塞满灰烬。
死神经过她走出来，如满面尘埃的运煤工，
重新折叠运尸袋，整理他的货物，
空袋叠着空袋，在一阵

尘埃和引擎转速的慌乱中，但此刻
是哪辆卡车？年轻的阿格纽的，还是另一辆，
更沉重，更致命，在她死后，
定时爆炸在马拉费尔特……
那就点数袋子并对黑夜甜言蜜语吧，运煤工。
聆听雨滴落入新的灰烬，

当你扛起马拉费尔特的尘埃，
再度从你的卡车中现身，我母亲的
梦中情人运煤工，在丝绸白的灰烬中出镜。

西 梅

纹章红，水泥灰。暗沉未干的血
在泥瓦匠的指节，像西梅汁
渗透他打包的午餐。
　　　　　　满满的砖斗
靠着灰浆墙，明晃晃的大抹刀
在他左手中（仅此一次），刀锋向下，
他对右手感到惊讶，高高举起，又红又疼：
城堡之王，登脚手架的人，
流血示众。
　　　　　　我五十年前
看到的血色黏稠的伤口——
西梅如预兆，古怪，待解之梦——
正与一臂之遥的死者一同哭泣，
他们来自各处及无处，此时此地。

　　　　　　　　　　*

一遍又一遍，粉刷，刮擦，混合，
他反复涂抹又涂抹，铺好
一层层阴郁的灰浆。然后砖块

颤颤巍巍放稳，叮叮当当对齐。

我尤其爱那抹刀的光亮，

刀刃和刀锋永远洁净

并在泥水中明亮自身。

它看着很轻却像武器一样重，

而他毫不费力就把它举起。

整个过程就是填缝、撇净、浮动和反光

直到他把它洗净并裹进麻布袋，

如同异教徒的刀，必须隐藏。

*

鬼魂伸出舌头舔一口血，

挤在梯子上，全都未愈，

有些还穿着带血的衣服。

把它们送回门阶或路上，

它们曾在那儿躺在自己的血里，

在灼热的眩晕和宝贵生命的最后喘息里。

挥舞抹刀的人啊，受伤的兄弟，把它们赶走

如同奥德修斯在冥府挥刀

舞剑，挖出一条壕沟并割断

献祭羊羔的咽喉。

　　　　　但又不像他——

建筑工，而非洗劫者，你的盾牌是灰浆板——

载它们回家，回到酒红色的美味，

回到西梅在锅里煨炖的芳香，

舀起浓稠的果酱，在阳光下蒸腾。

施　压

五十六磅的砝码。铁打的
否定单位。压印铸刻着
套印小图，厚如梯级，模制，短梁

提手。摆好阵势，看似无害
直到你试图抬起它，接着是让人脱臼、
贬低生命的力量——

引力的黑匣，任你跺脚、蹲下
都无法移动那重负的平方根。
但用另一个

砝码去平衡它，把它们放上地秤——
一个调试好的、新上过油的地秤——
然后一切颤抖，互相妥协。

*

这就是一切福音的意义：
忍耐的原则，在忍耐中振作，

在忍耐中支撑，无非是不得不

用他人身上之不可忍
来平衡我们自己的，不得不遵守
我们勉强接受并习惯的一切，

无论是否违心。消极
受苦让世界运转。
天下太平，人人好心，这一切

要奏效，就必须保持平衡，
让天平稳定，让天使的旋律
在超凡绝尘的音高上延长。

*

拒绝伸出另一边脸。抛石头。
有时不这么做，不与你自我伤害
而成为的逆来顺受者决裂

就是辜负那伤害、自我和内在的法则。
预言谁会打你！当士兵们戏弄
被蒙上眼睛的耶稣时，他不还手。

160

他们不觉羞耻也未受教化，尽管

有些事不言自明——不行使力量的

力量，永远由弱者间接

表达的希望。不过，看在耶稣的分上，

帮我个忙，仅此一次，好吗？

预言，立恶表，抛石头。[①]

*

每个问题都有两面，是，是，是……

但有些时候，仅仅施加压力

就是必要的基本原则，无需

任何自我开脱或自哀自怜。

唉，一晚，当有必要战斗到底，

一个快速出击就能将对方击溃，

[①] 本诗中的"另一边脸"，预言（谁会打你），立恶表，抛石头，
都出自圣经典故。"另一边脸"，出自《马太福音》，耶稣说："有
人打你的右脸，把左脸也转过去。""预言谁会打你"，出自《路
加福音》："看守耶稣的人戏弄他、殴打他，又蒙住他的眼睛问
他说：'你说预言吧，打你的是谁？'"立恶表，立恶榜样，引
人犯罪，典出《马太福音》。抛石头，《约翰福音》中关于通奸女
人被罚、将被乱石砸死的故事，耶稣说："你们当中谁没有罪，
谁就先用石头砸她吧。"

你反驳说，正是我的偏狭

让我始终尖锐，所以先输一局。

本该让对方流血时我却退缩，

就那样（我的错）失去优势。

深受误解的骑士精神，老朋友。

此时此刻，唯有不公擦净石板。[①]

---

① 擦净石板（clean the slate），比喻原谅过去的错误，忘却以往
的冒犯，重新开始。

圣凯文与黑鸟 ^①

然后是圣凯文与黑鸟。
圣徒跪着，手臂伸展，在他的
斗室，斗室狭小，所以

一只手掌心朝上伸出窗外，僵直
如横梁，这时一只黑鸟在他掌中
栖落、生蛋并安家筑巢。

凯文感觉着温热的蛋，小小的胸脯，蜷缩
而整洁的小脑袋和小爪，感到自己
被接入永恒生命的网络，

感动悲悯：现在他必须把手伸出
如树枝，连续数周无论晴雨，
直到小鸟孵出、羽翼渐丰，然后飞离。

---

① 圣凯文（St Kevin，498–613），爱尔兰圣徒，他在威克洛郡
建立了格伦达洛（Glendalough）修道院。他与黑鸟的故事广为
流传。

*

而既然整个故事都出自想象，
想象你是凯文。他是哪一种？
忘却自我还是终日痛苦，

从脖颈直到疼痛的小臂？
他的手指睡着了吗？他还能感觉到膝盖吗？
还是地下的盲然无觉已经

爬上他全身？他的意识中拉开距离了吗？
独自并清晰地倒映在爱的深河，
"但问耕耘，莫求收获，"他祈祷，

他完完全全用身体去做的祈祷，
因为他已经忘了自己，忘了鸟儿，
在河岸上忘了河的名字。

航　线

一

先对折，然后再折几次
每一次都更紧密更整齐
直到整张纸缩小为
一个多褶的方块，他会拎起两角，
然后仿佛握住一个他有能力打破
而从未那样做的承诺。

　　　　　　　一只鸽子在我心中飞起，
每当我父亲的双手和盘托出
一条纸船，空中方舟，
线条拉紧像用木桩固定的帐篷：
高高的船尾，伸展的龙骨，中央
小小的金字塔完全中空
就像我的一部分，沉没，因为我知道
一旦你让它下水，整条船就会泡烂。

二

相等且相反，那部分^①升入

那些满天星斗的冬日苍穹，

当我在威克洛，站在从都柏林

飞来的夜班飞机航线下，它升起的灯光

在它拖行的机身前方闪烁：

巨大的引擎噪声和它的渐弱

远远铺展在后方，在下界，星光间的航迹。

梧桐在黑暗中说着梧桐语，

我肩后的光亮是村舍的灯火。

傍晚时分我待在门口，

我自己就是所有以同样姿态

定格之人的替身：留守者，

倚着门框翘首以盼；

我们挥别或归来时方知

深爱的人，不同的衣衫

使他们稍作迟疑。

　　　　　没有一次忘记

一个名或一张脸，也没有在飞机

---

① 呼应上一首诗中的"我的一部分"。

攀升至巡航高度时才突然往下看，
发现他们刚刚掠过的房子——
现已远得看不见——正是一小时前
他们离开的那所，当出租车司机装好行李，
他们还在那里亲吻，亲吻。

三

升空并远去。免税店的嗡鸣。
黑丝绒^①。波本酒。空中情书。
曼哈顿太空漫步。重新返回。

然后是加州。放松的蒂布龙。
山姆的汉堡，户外餐桌和香槟，
还有白眼的烤干的海鸥在旁观。

再次重返。重新立誓。然后离开——
以退为进，在归来后的
一年，更像暂歇而非长别。

那么去格兰摩尔，格兰摩尔，格兰摩尔。
在困境，在适应，在劳作，在历险并确定。

---

① 黑丝绒，指爱尔兰鸡尾酒。

丛林与家园。橡树、月桂与梧桐。

接着坐飞机。穿越，穿越，穿越。
向西，向东，飞机成了校车，
"庭院"①是农舍与校园的混合物。

等待航线并牢牢抓紧——
斯威尼迷失于贺拉斯的逆耳忠言：
渡海者改变环境而非心境。

四

以下文字用于记录，鉴于
此前和此后的一切：
一个明媚的五月清晨，一九七九年，
刚从纽约飞来的红眼专机上下来，
我坐火车前往贝尔法斯特。回家
当然很兴奋：斯凯里斯的
大海，婚庆的山楂花，
北方之旅像链条甜蜜地抓住
每一个实在的链齿。

         然后出场——

---

① 原文是 "The Yard"，指哈佛大学。

他仿佛某部黑色电影里的边防警察——
出场的是我在上一次梦中见过的人，
此刻他比梦里更阴郁，
当他在山路旁招呼我下车，
走过来把胳膊肘架在车顶，
透过敞开的车窗解释，
我要做的全部就是小心翼翼
驾驶一辆面包车前往佩蒂戈的
下一个关卡，熄火，下车，就好像
我是去办事处交报关单——
但实际上我还要多走十码
来到大街上与一个人接头——这是
另一个校友的名字，眨眼微笑，
我会立刻认出他来，他将开一辆福特
而不出三小时，我便回到家，绝对
安全……
　　　　　于是他进来坐在
我对面，劈头质问。
"他妈的看在上天分上，你什么时候
为我们写点东西？""如果我真写，
不管写什么，我都为我自己写。"
就这样。或类似的意思。

那几个月里监狱墙上涂着粪。

在肮脏抗议后走出长凯奇，

红眼是基尔伦·纽金特①的眼睛，

像从但丁那污浊的地狱里走出的东西，

一路钻探，穿过韵律和意象，在那里

我也曾走在正直的维吉尔身后，

绝对安全并自由翻译：

说完这一切，他的眼珠骨碌，

他的牙齿，如犬牙咬紧尸骨，

咬入头颅并再度紧紧咬住。

五

当我回答说我来自"远方"，

关卡的警察厉声问，"那是哪里？"

他只听见我的半句话，就以为

那是国家北部的某个地区。

而现在它——既是我一直居住

---

① 基尔伦·纽金特（Ciaran/Kieran Nugent，1958–2000），长凯奇即梅兹监狱中第一个进行"毯子示威"的爱尔兰共和军人员。犯人们自视为政治犯，却被当局当作一般犯人处置，使之失去政治犯的特权。纽金特率先采取行动，拒绝穿囚服，用毯子将自己裹起来，其他犯人效仿。英国当局毫不退让。由于必须穿囚服才分发厕纸，犯人们就把粪便涂在监狱墙壁上，史称"肮脏抗议"。

也是我已离开之地——还有很长的路要走，

像星光，花了多少光年才从远方走来

还要多少光年才能抵达归宿。

六

于是出人意料地，纯粹的兴奋

是忆起之字形登上温暖的台阶，

前往罗卡马杜尔上方那隐士的巢穴。

乌鸦飞得又高又近，蜥蜴

在我脚边的沙砾上搏动，前腿

像月球车前方尖尖的支架。

大大地，柔柔地，如一息微风里的

生命气息，一只青橙绿蝴蝶

穿过朝圣者暴晒下的"苦路"。

上午十一点钟。我写下笔记：

"爱岩者，孤独者，空中哨所，万福！"

然后鸽子从某处飞起。并持续飞升。

招　魂

靠近我，麦克迪尔米德①，从舍特兰，

因凝视石头而目光如石，酒醒

而暴躁。不是炉火旁那个

老治安员，整天就知道哄我们，

逗我们，酒鬼中的酒鬼；不，

靠近我，智者，藐视礁石的风，

停于海风的鸥，躲在鸟儿视线后

看守敞开之门的守门人——

不要听我收回嘲讽的话，

说你具有麦克贡纳格尔②倾向——

因为我不会——但中年的我要补充说：

我低估了你前卫而滔滔不绝的天才。

———————————

① 休·麦克迪尔米德（Hugh MacDiarmid，1892-1978），诗人，
苏格兰文艺复兴的领袖，民族主义者。
② 麦克贡纳格尔（William Topaz McGonagall，1825-1902），苏
格兰的平庸诗人。

*

特别是在海景房那些年。
更像智慧的雄山羊而非替罪羊，
超越石头的界限，下笔如狂。

久经考验的骄傲。孤寂。
窗玻璃上你苍白的大脑门
如大地的弧线映在大海朝北的弧线。

那时你茫然若失，却始终忙于
往返海滩，在地平线和字典
之间测定烈性的方位，

走在老问题和老答案的岩面，
持强硬路线者，我再问一句：
"谁是我的邻居？我的邻居是全人类。"

*

而假若你不靠近，那么保持
拥抱的距离。做那只小小的
风雨鸫，就像你一直如此，

像观察风云那样观察风云般的诗歌，
一种变化之力，一个被分解的因子
无论是否占上风，始终都是

它所处的时间与地点的函数，
有时也在我们的。但无论如何绝不
在我们之外，即使有时怪异。

在口音里，在习语里，在
思想里犹如风中的一朵蓟，
一个永远值得重申的训诫。

休·麦克迪尔米德（1892–1978）

迈锡尼守望者

公牛在我舌上。

——埃斯库罗斯,《阿伽门农》

1. 守望者的战争

有些人哭了,不是悲伤——而是高兴

因为国王终于披甲纵身驶向特洛伊,

但我内心就像敲锣打鼓,

依然预见并忍耐那杀人的聚会,

及其导致的生命扭曲和世界不公。

我梦见浅滩上明亮蛛网里的血,

梦见尸体像碎肉倾盆落在

我熟睡的身上——而我是

女王下令设岗又遗忘的守望者,

是她的远见所依赖的盲点。

然后公牛会压在锣上

为它消音,而我会感到我的舌头

就像运牛货车放下的跳板,

遭受践踏，发出响声，屎尿横流，
摇曳颤抖如一条火舌，
屠宰场里的胜利烽火……
接着我会在茫然中醒来，
完全像一只躺在草丛里的牧羊犬，
暴露于我所知道的真相，依然为了
荣誉将注意力集中在远处，
越过城邦和边境，聚焦那条线，
当特洛伊沦陷，烽火会跃上群山。

我的哨兵工作是宿命，是归宿，
是年复一年我必须划船越渡的
中游时间：当茫茫迷雾开始
在田野与河湾上散去，当晨光
敞开，仿佛光的纹理被撕裂，
日复一日，我又重新活过来，
沉寂且暴晒如平原上的蛇丘，
支撑在我的双肘上，凝望，等待时机，
在我屋顶的前哨……十年战争的
漫长等待导致的结果无非是
让我黑镜般冻结的凝视失去光泽。
如果一个正义之神从天上伸下手来
摸索一根更结实的秤杆挂他的秤盘
他会发现我蓄势待发并准备就绪。

我在命运和恐惧之间维持平衡，

看到它来了，云彩布满血丝，

那是胜利的红焰，黎明的红肿

伤口引燃并爆发，汩汩喷涌

像熔岩淹没逃跑的人群……

支撑在我的双肘上，头向后，挡住

克吕泰涅斯特拉痛苦的爱欲尖叫，

那声音响彻宫殿如阿伽门农国王

从船舰上驱逐的军队发出的叫嚣。

2. 卡珊德拉

没有清白

旁观

这回事。

她污浊的胸衣，

她小小的乳房，

她被剪短的、荒

芜的、结痂的

朋克头，

炭黑的眼睛

饥饿的呆望——
她看起来
曾被反复蹂躏

并单纯。
人们
能感到

一种缺失的
真实在她眼中
聚焦，

一种返乡
在她低垂的翅膀，
半精明的

迷惑。
没有清白
这回事。

称王称霸的
老国王
回来了，

杀孩子

见什么

抢什么的

国王

阿伽门农王

勃起的

老雄兽的

阔步又回来了。

然后她的希腊

语词也来了，

一只羊羔

在产羊羔时，

咩咩发出

先知的恐惧，

传宗锤

和愤怒之神的

脚步。

以及由此产

生的惊人欲望

即旁观者

想要干她

就在那时那地。

他们的罪行，

小小的阴部裂口：

她进去

走向刀，

走向杀人妻，

走向盖着

她和她的奴隶主

特洛伊劫掠者的网，

说道："海绵

一抹，

如此而已。

影子铰链

摇摆不

定而光

已熄灭。"

3. 他的黎明幻象

草的城。堡垒墙。惊愕的宫殿。
我醒来时晚风拂面，
好奇，再度警觉，但远远

不如我该有的那样关注胜利——
依然因为一贯藐视谄媚者
而受到孤立，那些人总是需要作为

真正的阿尔戈斯人被看见被听见。嘴巴运动员，
引用神谕并引用日期，
申诉，指控，投票表决。

没有任何有力的元素
能够移译那悲伤的过往。
我们的战争哑口无言。

紫罗兰在花茎上垂下小小脑袋，

黎明前的游丝，露珠、纱幔

与星状蕾丝，我更多是透过它们

感受我们身处其中的时代重创的

脉搏。我的灵魂在我掌中啜泣，

当我触碰它们，我整个生命倾盆

落在我身上，我看见草的城，

企盼谷，坟墓，被风吹拂的明亮，

而远处，在一个多山、不祥的地方，

三三两两的人群看一个男人

跃过一堵新的土墙，另一个

多情地奔跑，仿佛，要把他打倒。

4. 夜 夜

他们俩都需要交谈，

假装他们需要的是

我的忠告。背地里

他们各自坦言

每次他们做，

都是性爱的超负荷——
而且确实从一开始
（即使孩子也不会无视）
他们真正的生活就是床。

国王本应知道，
但谁去告诉他呢，
如若不是我？我劝他们
停止，并打破我守口
如瓶的别有用心的沉默，
但依然如故，每天早晨
对埃癸斯托斯满脸堆笑，
既受恩宠又自我厌恶。
屋顶如一个耳鼓。

公牛保持无尽的哑默
懒惰，垂头
不动如石柱。
阿特拉斯，守望者的保护神，
会进入我脑海，
他是唯一另一个
时刻警觉的人，像公牛那样俯身
在他的云轭下，
在世界的尽头。

诸男神和女神

无数次成功与

情人幽会的阁楼，

穿过云层传来的

砰砰和呻吟

全都压在他肩头。

有时我想象我们

被神化为巨砾，

被唤作阿芙洛狄忒支柱。

那些日子，高潮与低潮

都渐入佳境。

当木马里的官兵

感到海伦的手抚摸

它的木板和肚子

他们几乎骑上彼此。

结果特洛伊的母亲们

首当其冲，在巷口，

在血染的婴儿车和成人床。

战争把所有男人都逼疯，

戴绿帽，藏木马或守屋顶，

耀武威并吃败仗。

我的心是一间候审室

那里戴绿帽的阿伽门农王

用黄金打造他的威望。

然而当群山失火，

王后哀嚎跑来，

我出卖的是国王。

我不只是不忠：

因为他的金条，他的奖赏

是一个绳网，一场血洗。

于是和平降临我们。

5. 他对水的遐思

在特洛伊，在雅典，我最清楚地

看见并几乎闻见的

是清新的水。

一个注满的浴缸，尚未被涉足，

尚未被污染，等在屋墙后，

平原上被屠杀者的遥远呼声

不断消逝在墙垣，直到那位英雄

不可思议地降临，
被侍候，单独地，

被脱光，血迹斑斑，呻吟
摇晃，泼溅，瞌睡，
仿佛他是陌生人。

还有雅典的井泉。
不如说那条曲曲折折
从卫城通往井泉的

古老生命线，一组木阶
嵌入陡峭的崖壁和一堵
独立、掩护的岩石之间，

秘密的楼梯，防御者知晓，
入侵者找到，在那里，
希腊的未来遇见希腊人，

未来与过去、
围攻者与被围者的梯子，
进攻的阶梯

化为辘轳，秘密的梯级和

习惯的梯级都是同一只
赤脚伸出、求索，

然后我们自己的梯子深深坠入
正在光天化日之下被开掘的
竖井，男人们身陷源头

褐色的淤泥，再走上来时
自身也因置身那里而变得深沉，
如退伍的士兵测试安全的地面，

清水的发现者，守护者，预见者，
来自铁水泵和水喷头的
丰饶圆嘴。

给辛西娅和德米特里·哈吉

最初的词语

最初的词语被污染了

就像早晨的河水

流淌着广告文案

和头版头条的灰尘。

我唯一的饮品是脑海深处的意义,

是鸟儿、青草和石头所畅饮的。

就让一切逆流而上

流向四大元素,

流向地水火风。

改写自马林·索列斯库的罗马尼亚语诗歌

砾石路

河水中的砾石。起初，那样。
盛夏，垂钓者的摩托车
深埋在路边花丛，像一位倒下的骑士，
我们才问过他的鬼魂。"运气如何？"

当世界的引擎准备就绪，绿坚果
在离旋涡更近的地方摇曳、聚集。
树木低垂。燧石和砂岩碎片
在闪亮的麦芽糖色的浅浅急流中

把自己磨得更滑更小，那里
成群的米诺鱼被我们的嬉戏吓跑——
一种永恒告终，一旦拖拉机
在砾石河床卸下它的挂斗，

混凝土搅拌机也开始苏醒，
穿粗布工装裤的人们，像被俘的鬼魂，
搅拌水泥、装货、滚动、旋转、滚动，仿佛
法老的砖厂在他们脑中燃烧。

*

珍藏并赞美这砾石的真理。
不惑者的宝石。大地的鱼白。
它与铁锹撞击时那朴素的磨牙之歌
为"诚实价值"这类词语试音并喷砂。

在河水内外都是美的，
这砾石的王国也在你内部——
在深底，在远处，清澈的河水流过
焦糖、冰雹和鲭鱼蓝的卵石。

但那实际被冲刷的东西让你平缓
当你躬身推着满载的手推车
进入一种肉体的赦免，
疲惫的骨头和骨髓感到被救赎的生命。

那么漫步空中，不顾一切，
在批量生产的坚硬混凝土
与绿意盎然的乐曲《砾石路》
之间确立你自己的位置。

默尤拉河上的惠特比

凯德蒙[①]，我也有幸认识他，

他回到原地，带着满满的水桶

和一抱抱干净的稻草，完美的农夫，

漫不经心地做着他分内的事，

但做得完美，并且打量你。

他发挥了他天使的潜质。他像钉子一样硬

且终日在那里用竖琴赋诗

但他真正的天赋是依然能发出

粗鲁的吼声，当他热情地投入劳动

仿佛那些神圣的话题是一群

溃散并需要被驱拢的牲口。

我从来没有一次看见他合掌，

除非当他把目光投向天堂；

还有当他快速嗅闻并测试

拂过病兽尿液的指尖时。

哦，凯德蒙的确是真货色。

---

① 凯德蒙（Caedmon），七世纪盎格鲁-撒克逊僧侣、诗人，据说原本是不识字的牧人，在梦中获得灵感，写下以圣经为主题的诗篇。

顶　针

一

在情色壁画厅①
画家用它来维持一种特殊的红
那是他画嘴唇和新咬痕时用的颜色。

二

直到宗教改革前，它一直被尊为
圣阿达曼的遗物。
工匠们在某个铸造坊
铸一口钟，那么重，据说，
没有设备能把它抬上钟楼——
随后，工匠们一个接一个
染上一种嗜睡症。
在浇铸金属时火红的
精神错乱中，他们全都安静下来
并看到绿水草和踏脚石
布满熔化的青铜。

———————————
① 指庞贝壁画。

192

于是阿达曼来了，祝福他们的双手

和眼睛，并治愈他们，但在那一时刻

那口钟也神奇地缩小了，

从此它就为虔诚的信徒所知

并载入修士的名物，

史称阿达曼的顶针。

三

这就是最甜蜜誓言的韵味吗，

蘸湿的饥渴画笔，天堂的甘露，

他们才说"一顶针"①，就从我舌间跑掉？

四

现在的少年

剃光头

裸肩

把它当乳贴。

五

诸如此类。

---

① 指极少量。

黄油印花板

谁在黄油印花板的圆脸上刻下
黑麦的花穗，满是尖刺和胡须？
为什么柔软的黄油要印上那样尖锐的图案
仿佛用碎玻璃片割划它的胸脯？

小时候我曾吞下黑麦的芒刺。
我的咽喉就像直立的庄稼被镰刀刺探。
我感觉它的边缘滑下而尖梢卡在深处
直到，我咳了又咳才把它咳出来，

我的呼吸像黎明一样冷，那么清爽并突然，
我很可能是吸入了天堂的空气，
被治愈的殉道者阿加莎从上方俯瞰，
盯着那把圣物刀，就像我盯着麦芒。

记忆中的石柱

尘世的坚固字母变得轻盈。
大理石衬线字体，压印清晰的立柱
建于岩石之上并屹立群山之巅，
像记忆中故事里的石柱升起，

从前，圣母的房舍腾空飞起，
降落在洛雷托的山顶。
在眩晕的信条中我举目远望
发现移译中幸存的真实不虚。

《诗人椅》

给卡罗琳·马尔霍兰[①]

列奥纳多说，太阳从未
见过阴影。瞧这位雕塑家围绕
她的下一件作品转了整整一圈，像恋人
在变换角度与恒定之爱的范围里。

一

在这阳光追踪的城中庭院
你的诗人椅要面对并超越的
正是它自身变化角度的阴影。
始终保持警觉，四只腿落在
它们的脚上——猫脚，山羊脚，大而软的八字脚；
它挺直的椅背上长出两支青铜的繁茂嫩枝。
城里每一个饶舌者，
老太婆和酒鬼，深夜撒尿的、亲吻的，
都愿意在它上面坐一会儿。
那是因为他们身后的风振奋而饱满，

---

① 卡罗琳·马尔霍兰（Carolyn Mulholland，1944– ），爱尔兰
雕塑家，她在一九八八年创作了诗中所写的椅子雕塑。

嫁接的嫩枝抓住他们的肩胛骨，
这些让他们高兴。一旦脱离大自然，
它们将在树叶、花朵和天使的脚步中
重返。或诸如此类的事物。那该死的
椅子长出了树叶！你信吗？

二

接着我看见白牢房里的椅子，
苏格拉底坐在上面，秃顶如秧鸡，
在明亮的阳光下与朋友们交谈。
他的时间不多了。他的审判开始那天，
一条碧绿的小船从提洛岛上的
阿波罗神庙驶来，参加一年一度的
纪念仪式。在花环与藤蔓
装点的船索重新进入雅典的
海港前，这座城的生活是神圣的。
没有处决。没有毒芹碗。没有眼泪
并且此时也没有，当毒药奏效
而职业狱吏在麻醉的每个阶段
都和围观的人们聊天。苏格拉底
在这座城的中心，而那天
证明了灵魂不朽。青铜树叶
不能相信它们的耳朵，如此沉寂。

很快，克里托将不得不闭上他的眼和口，

但此时此刻一切都是被延迟、

预知、想象且最为真实的疼痛。

三

我父亲在犁一、二、三、四面

耕地，我坐在田野中央，把一切

尽收眼底，背对那棵他们

永远不砍的山楂树。马儿全都只见马蹄

和光亮的肋腹，我对一切先知先觉。

比如诗歌如犁铧把时光

翻垦。比如奇幻的山楂树

进入茂叶椅迎接未来。

比如永远在此，在一切意义上。

秋 千

指尖轻轻一触就能把你送上
高空——一旦你已荡起来——
不亚于背后用力的推动。

                或早或晚，
我们一个个都学会荡上高天，
在露天的谷仓里荡来荡去，
用脚尖推，用力划，弯身穿过空气。

*

不是弗拉戈纳尔。也不是勃鲁盖尔。更像
汉斯·梅姆林①的天堂之光映在碧草地，
光映在田野和树篱，谷仓入口
在阳光照耀下满怀期待，褥草
堆在一旁，像一幅基督诞生图，
前景和背景等待人物出场。

---

① 让-奥诺雷·弗拉戈纳尔（Jean-Honoré Fragonard, 1732–1806），
法国画家，代表作有《秋千》《读书的少女》。彼得·勃鲁盖尔
（Pieter Brueghel，约 1525–1569），尼德兰画家。汉斯·梅姆林
（Hans Memling，1430–1494），尼德兰佛兰德斯画家。

然后，在画面中央，是秋千本身，

一个旧麻袋斜斜挂在它的索套上，

完美地静止，垂在那里如松弛的滑轮，

一个低垂的诱惑为诱使灵魂升扬。

*

即便如此，我们还是喜欢荡向大地。

她坐在那儿，威严如女皇，

把她浮肿的脚，一次一只，

放入搪瓷盆，并时不时地

用身旁地上那只水壶

给它浇灌丰饶而蒸腾的

弧线。对于我们的耳朵，那水声

是音乐，她的微笑是安慰。

无论女神出浴时以何种

光芒照耀她的心上人

都是此时所需：本该有

清新的亚麻布，侍从们的服侍，

仪仗队和惊叹声。相反，她拿来

每一只卷曲的弹力袜，把它穿上，

如同她不想放弃也别无选择的

生活。一次，当她洗净水盆，

她来坐在秋千上，为了取悦我们，
没有不合时宜，也并非她的日常，
只是一时兴起被它诱惑，
似乎重拾什么，似乎依然迷惑。
我们本能地知道不打扰、随她去。

*

要自己荡秋千，你把绳子拴在
背后，再向后倚靠并拉伸
直到绳子绷紧，然后踮起脚尖，尽可能
用力前冲。你把自己小小背上
积聚的一团重量抛入空中。
你低着头，你听见整个谷仓嘎吱作响。

*

我们一个个都学会荡上高天。
然后镇区消失，成为机场，
广岛的火光令人骨轻若无物，
协和式飞机的鼻尖移向未来。
所以，我们谁还想悬在那秋千上，
不顾一切？

        不顾一切，我们摇荡，

荡出自己之外，荡得更远更高，

高过我们肩胛骨里疼痛的房椽，

高过我们手臂间互相拉扯的枝条。

白 杨

风撼动大白杨，像水银
一下子让整棵树颤抖发光。
什么明亮的秤盘落下，指针颤动？
什么负载的天平令人绝望？

两幅手杖素描

一

克莱尔·奥雷利用她奶奶的手杖——
一个曲颈杖——去捕捞最高的荆棘，
那儿总是长着最熟的黑莓。
说起采集，珀耳塞福涅①
就远不如克莱尔那样幸运。
她会擅闯并爬过闸门，走上铁轨，
在那里，煤屑绽放为旋花，
火车疾驰而过，伴着司炉工的呼号，
像金戈铁马上受挫的国王。

二

摆放着牲口棍、黑刺李手杖和桴杖，
我父亲汽车后座的窗台
成了某种手杖店的橱窗，
但唯一浏览过商店橱窗的人

---

① 古希腊神话里的冥后。从小被母亲阻止与男性往来，却在采花时被冥王拐走。

是垂下巴的吉姆，因为吉姆头脑简单，

无论晴雨他都没完没了地绕来绕去，

从挡风玻璃到后窗，双手举到

他的两颊旁，一边窥探一边嘟囔。

所以会不时拿出那些手杖

给他看，把它们一根根

靠在车前的挡泥板上；吉姆

会一根根打量它们，瞄准、

挥舞、切割、刺戳并抵挡

并未造成妨碍的空气；直到他在

其中一根里找到自己的延伸，

而这让他欣喜若狂。他奔跑欢呼，

俯身向前，伸出他的右手肘，

夹住与地面平行的手杖，

倾斜地横在他前方，仿佛

他被它拴着，它牵着他走

像一根势不可当的车辕。

电　话

"别挂断，"她说，"我这就跑去找他。
今天天气特别好，他趁机
去除一点草。"
　　　　　　于是我看见他
趴着跪在那道葱垄旁，
抚摸，检查，分开彼此
缠结的茎叶，温柔地拔起
所有未成形的纤弱无叶的秧苗，
很高兴每一株小小的杂草都连根折断，
但也感到怜悯……

　　　　　　然后我发现自己聆听着
客厅钟表被扩音而凝重的嘀嗒，
电话被孤零零地搁在那儿，平静地
待在镜子和阳光照耀的钟摆旁……

然后发现自己在想：换作如今，
这就是死神召唤凡人的方式。

然后他说话，而我几乎说出我爱他。

差 使

"快去！儿子，像魔鬼那样拼命跑，
去告诉你妈妈，让她尝试
帮我找一个酒精水准仪的气泡
再给这领带打一个新结。"

但他还是很高兴，我知道，当我原地不动，
坚决与他对抗，
用一个微笑驳倒他的微笑和他那傻瓜的差使，
等待游戏的下一步。

今晚威克洛也有一只狗在叫

纪念多纳图斯·恩沃加[①]

当人类刚刚发现死亡这回事，

他们派一只狗去给楚库捎信：

他们希望被放归生的家园。

他们不想一死百了、永远消失

如同焚烧的木头化为烟云

或如灰烬被吹散化为乌有。

相反，他们看见灵魂是黄昏的鸟群，

啼鸣并飞回从前同样的栖息处，

同样明快的歌唱，每天清晨舒展翅膀。

死亡就像在树林中度过一夜：

破晓他们就回到生的家园。

（他们希望狗把这一切告诉楚库。）

然而死亡和人类都是次要的

当它从路上跑开，光天化日下

---

① 多纳图斯·恩沃加（Donatus Nwoga，1933–1991），尼日利亚
学者；五十年代，希尼在贝尔法斯特女王大学时的同学。恩沃
加根据尼日利亚的传说，改写了伊格博人（生活在尼日利亚东
南部的部族）的寓言，讲述了人类必死这一不可逆转的状态。
楚库（Chukwu）是他们信仰的最高神灵。

朝着另一只狗叫，那狗也从
远处河岸上回应它的叫声。

这就是为什么癞蛤蟆先找到楚库，
癞蛤蟆从一开始就偶然听到
狗要捎的口信。"人类，"他说，
（这里癞蛤蟆得到绝对信任）
"人类希望死亡永垂不朽。"

然后楚库看见人们的灵魂呈鸟形，
如夕阳下的黑点朝他飞来，
飞往一个无栖处也无树木、
更无路返回生之家园的地方。
他心里立即火冒三丈，
而无论狗后来告诉他什么，
都无法改变那图景。伟大的酋长和伟大的爱
消失于被遗忘的光，癞蛤蟆陷入淤泥，
狗彻夜在停尸房后嚎叫。

M.

当失聪的语音学家摊开他的手掌

抚摸一个说话者的头顶

他能通过骨骼的震动分辨出

说的是哪个双元音和哪个元音。

地球仪停止转动。我把手掌

放在永冻层般冰冷的轮廓，

想象转动轴的嗡鸣

和奥西普·曼德尔施塔姆坚定的俄语。

建筑师 ①

他在他天才的门阶上斋戒，

苟求更多，留意圆石

和打理过的枯山水。但也绝非懦夫，

无论何时畅饮威士忌，无论

独酌还是与别人豪饮。

永远彬彬有礼，永远着迷，令人惊异，

比如那天在海滨，他脱下衣服

在我们旁边赤身涉水，

陷入沉思，睿智而高挑，

在他乐土般的阔步中举重若轻，

闲谈把他带回现场和真相，

那是建筑艺术的必需，也是他的生活必需：

青石板和白石灰，阴影线，投影，

---

① 罗宾·沃克（Robin Walker, 1924-1991），爱尔兰杰出建筑师。

既显明又透明的事物。

勾勒，细描，延长，重绘，历历在目……

此刻离去，穿着粗花呢，沿着两侧
画板林立的通道，直至目光所及，
直至目光之外，除非他画出那里。

磨刀石

在我们二手买来的一只

香松木药剂师抽屉柜里，

一个重重的抽屉深处，

我发现这块磨刀石，原本是

我们送他①的礼物。还裹着包装纸。

像一个我未能递出的接力棒，闪耀黑光。

＊

不通风的灰烬深处。但尽管如此，

它躺在那里，也唤醒一些事……

我想起我们在圆木上的那晚，

平躺着，我们俩，平行，

从头到脚，胳膊伸直，目光直视，

倾听雨从树上落下的声音，

什么都不说，牢牢钉在潮湿的树皮上。

我们俩着了什么魔？光秃秃，无枝叶，

两根可爱的冬日树干，它们仿佛准备好

_____

① 指希尼的岳父。

下水，与一条矮篱笆桩围起的堤道

呈直角，如同滚筒一般。

我们都不说话。水潭静候。

工人们回家，锯子沉默。

然后我们躺着，林中的孩子，

仰望天空滂沱的雨脸，

直到一场大雨仿佛把我们带出

森林公园，脚先出去，向前看，

走出十一月，走出中年，

一起，走远，渡过默伊尔海。

                    *

夫妻石棺。赤陶土。

伊特鲁里亚夫妻并肩

向左侧卧，丈夫用右手指着

什么并望向所指之处，

妻子在前，戴着耳环，辫长

及腰，性感而舒适。

他睁着眼，她白日梦，

她的右小臂和右手伸出，仿佛

她深沉的内在目光看见的某只鸟

会在那里筑巢。家庭

之爱，艺术家想，暖色与富足，

赤陶土的脆弱……

这就是他们呈现在彩色明信片上的样子。

（卢浮宫，古代艺术部）

那是我们以前寄给他的，在他的物件中重现。

*

他喜爱富于启迪的错误：他的西班牙孙子的

英语直译，为了感谢他的

乘船旅行："爷爷，那真是一场

超级棒的水上漫步。"的确，

他自己在空中漫步，尤其在

鳏居后更加频繁，而他体内的那个

小伙，那个曾向她求爱的运动员——

在赛跑中以胸撞线，跳过高高的横杠——

再次变得轻快。八十①行驶在

最崎岖的道路上，为定点越野赛马

和聚众打牌孤注一掷，

又一次"他开启狂放生涯"

并且蛮不在乎。像火车一样抽烟，

对除草剂不屑一顾。

调情，吹牛。让他的床铺着了火。

———————————————

① 双关，既指速度，也指年龄。

从梯子上滚落。学会使用微波炉。

*

那么，把抽屉放在雪融的清水上，
再把未曾使用的磨刀石放里面：
明年夏天将在一个河岸上发现它，
在那里，镰刀曾整夜挂在赤杨上，
除草人在刀锋上奏响黎明的谐谑曲，
他们的双臂就像竖琴手的，一只靠近，
另一只拂过最远处的明亮琴弦。

海　滩

我父亲的桦杖在桑迪芒特海滩

留下的点点线线

是海浪不会冲走的另一事物。

散 步

迷人的是路，日子，他和她以及

他们带我去过的所有地方。当我们外出散步，

鹅卵石就是河床，星期天的空气，

是高高的水帘，沉默地漂移在

盛开的杜鹃花、毛地黄、

毒芹、"树篱上的知更鸟"①、树篱

连同花边常春藤与浓密的阴影之上——

直到河床本身出现。

沙砾，浅滩，夏季池塘，

成为不可跨越的世界边缘。

爱领着我来到那么远，没有

丝毫怀疑或讥讽，干眼睛②，

有见识，也会可恶地作对；

于是就一直站在那儿，不松手。

---

① "树篱上的知更鸟"（robin-run-the hedge），植物，学名为原
拉拉藤（*Galium aparine*）。诗中紧接着出现 "树篱"（hedge）一
词，呼应着 "树篱上的知更鸟"，所以保留俗名直译。
② "干眼睛"，原文是 "dry-eyed"，指无泪，不哭，不多愁善感。

*

另一张远景照片。黑白。

这次是底片，耀目黑。

模糊与苍白中我们辨出你我，

我们与之挣扎并从中挣脱的自我，

吞噬彼此火苗的两个幽魂，

阳光下灼烫并烧焦的两道火焰，

但看上去就像缕缕无力的微风，

闪烁的余波，如羽的天空变幻……

但依然可能在一瞬间重燃

假如我们沿途发现烧焦的青草和树枝

以及一股缭绕不散的陈年火香，

爱欲的木柴烟，巫术，神秘，

并没有让我们更明智，只是更好地准备着

再次加速开垦并喂食火焰。

在源头

你的歌，当你一如既往闭着眼睛①

唱起它们，就像一条本地的小路，

我们曾知道它的每一处转弯——

蚊蚋笼罩、树篱高高的旁路，你站在那里

张望聆听，直到一辆汽车

来了又去，让你比开始歌唱时

更孤独。那么，继续唱吧，

亲爱的合眼人，亲爱的，声音杳远的老手，

唱吧，直至抵达歌唱的源头，

热烈而隔绝如我们的盲邻居

整天在她的卧室里弹钢琴。

她的音符传来如同提起的水

从水桶纷纷洒落在源头，

于是我们在那儿听，安静而笨拙。

---

① 此处的 "你" 指的是盲人音乐家罗茜·基南（Rosie Keenan）。

*

那位天生失明、嗓音甜美、孤僻的音乐家
就像沉重黏土里的银矿脉。
白昼之光里闪耀的黑夜水。
但也是我们的邻居，罗茜·基南。
她抚摸我们的脸蛋。她让我们触摸她的布莱叶盲文，
在似书非书的书本里，壁纸图案扑面。
她的手活跃而她的眼充满
敞开的黑暗和水灵的光亮。

她靠声音辨识我们。她会说她"看见"
谁或什么。和她在一起，
亲密而有益，像你不知不觉
发生的治愈。当我读起
写到基南的井的那首诗，她说，
"我现在能看见井底的天空。"

在巴纳赫

然后突然间出现在我面前，
那位上门裁缝，我的前身：
坐在桌上，盘着腿，撕开

一件他必须重新裁剪或重新缝纫的衣服，
他嘴唇紧闭，牙齿间有一根线，
永远隐藏自己的意图，更不给出意见，

眼睑坚定如皱盔犀鸟或熨铁。
自我疏离，流动而安顿；
被请进厨房，请进衣裳

他的触碰能让它再回归布料——
突然间他出现在我面前，
没有敞开，没有虚假，没被照亮。

*

那么祝他工作顺利，我的观察
使他很不自在，尽管多年来

他一直神秘莫测，当他穿针引线

或搭配镶边、衬里、褶边和接缝。
他举起针，偏离中心，眯起眼睛，
把线舔了又舔，并一下子穿进去，

然后不慌不忙地把两端对齐，
用力拨两下。接着继续缝合。
他可曾问过这一切有什么意义

或究竟会不会问起？或在意睡在哪里？
我巴纳赫的佛祖啊，大道
因你存在其中而更开阔。

图 伦

那个星期天早上我们走了很远。
我们长久地站在图伦沼泽。
那片低地，那乌黑的水，那浓密的草
既像幻觉又似曾相识。

一条穿过日德兰田野的小径。轻微的车辆声。
柳树丛；灯芯草；结实的沼泽杉
在打扫过的围栏农院；休眠的湿地。
层层包裹的青贮饲料在它沉默的堆垛里。

这很可能是一幅静物画，来自明亮的
《和平之乡》，关于梦幻农场的诗
无可争议。稻草人的手臂
张开，对着围场里的卫星

碟形天线，一块屹立的石头
被重新安置并成为景观，

游客指示牌上有北欧古字母如尼文[①]、
丹麦文和英文。时过境迁。

这很可能是马尔霍兰镇或斯克里布。
那些小路把名字写在白底黑字的
路牌；对游客友好的偏远地区，
在那里我们自由自在，如在家中远离宗派，

更像侦查员而非陌生人，在外游荡的鬼魂
不惧光亮，去迎接新的开始
并迎接成功，生而有罪，
回到我们自己，回归自由意志，不错。

一九九四年九月

---

① 如尼文：古代书写体系中的字母，属于日耳曼语族，在中世
纪的欧洲，特别是斯堪的纳维亚半岛与不列颠群岛使用。也叫
"卢恩字母"。今已消亡。

附　言

哪天花些时间开车往西
进入克莱尔郡，沿着鸢尾岸，
在九月或十月，那时秋风
与天光一齐发挥互补的功用，
以至于一边大海狂野，
浪花闪烁，而内陆砾石间，
一片石板灰的湖泊表面
被一群天鹅的接地闪电点燃，
它们羽毛凌乱，白叠着白，
一个个丰满而倔强的脑袋
蜷缩、昂起或在水下忙着。
想停下车更仔细地捕捉它
是没用的。你不在这里或那里，
只是匆匆而过，熟悉与陌生的事物都从中穿行，
当温柔的海风持续从侧方拍打着汽车，
倏然吹开猝不及防的心灵。

希尼在都柏林桑迪芒特码头，一九九六年（Bobbie Hanvey 摄）

Seeing Things

For Derek Mahon

Contents

Acknowledgements

Acknowledgements are due to the editors of the following, where some of these poems appeared for the first time: *Agenda*; *Agni Review*; *Antaeus*; *Belfast Newsletter*; *English Review*; *Field*; *Georgia Review*; *Irish Times*; *London Review of Books*; *Observer*; *Orbis*; *Owl*; *Oxford Gazette*; *Oxford Poetry*; *Parnassus*; *Ploughshares*; *Poetry Ireland*; *Poetry Review*; *Salmagundi*; *Stet*; *Sunday Tribune*; *Thames Poetry*; *The Threepenny Review*; *The Times Literary Supplement*; *Tikkun*; *Translation*.

The following were first published by *The New Yorker*: 'A Basket of Chestnuts', 'Crossings', Nos. xviii, xxx, xxxi, xxxii, xxxiii, xxxiv, xxxv, xxxvi.

A number of the poems in Part I were printed in *The Tree Clock* (Linen Hall Library, Belfast, 1990).

The Golden Bough

(*Aeneid*, Book VI, lines 98–148)

So from the back of her shrine the Sibyl of Cumae
Chanted fearful equivocal words and made the cave echo
With sayings where clear truths and mysteries
Were inextricably twined. Apollo turned and twisted
His spurs at her breast, gave her her head, then reined in
    her spasms.

As soon as her fit passed away and the mad mouthings stopped
Heroic Aeneas began: 'No ordeal, O Priestess,
That you can imagine would ever surprise me
For already I have foreseen and foresuffered all.
But one thing I pray for especially: since they say it is here
That the King of the Underworld's gateway is to be found,
Among these shadowy marshes where Acheron comes flooding
    through,
I pray for one look, one face-to-face meeting with my dear
    father.
Teach me the way and open the holy doors wide.
I carried him on these shoulders through flames
And thousands of enemy spears. In the thick of battle I
    saved him
And he was at my side then through all my sea-journeys,
A man in old age, worn out yet holding out always.
And he too it was who half-prayed and half-ordered me
To make this approach, to find and petition you.
So therefore, Vestal, I beseech you take pity
On a son and a father, for nothing is out of your power
Whom Hecate appointed the keeper of wooded Avernus.
If Orpheus could call back the shade of a wife through his
    faith
In the loudly plucked strings of his Thracian lyre,
If Pollux could redeem a brother by going in turns
Backwards and forwards so often to the land of the dead,

And if Theseus too, and great Hercules... But why speak of
    them?
I myself am of highest birth, a descendant of Jove.'

He was praying like that and holding on to the altar
When the prophetess started to speak: 'Blood relation of gods,
Trojan, son of Anchises, the way down to Avernus is easy.
Day and night black Pluto's door stands open.
But to retrace your steps and get back to upper air,
This is the real task and the real undertaking.
A few have been able to do it, sons of gods
Favoured by Jupiter the Just, or exalted to heaven
In a blaze of heroic glory. Forests spread midway down,
And Cocytus winds through the dark, licking its banks.
Still, if love torments you so much and you so much need
To sail the Stygian lake twice and twice to inspect
The murk of Tartarus, if you will go beyond the limit,
Understand what you must do beforehand.
Hidden in the thick of a tree is a bough made of gold
And its leaves and pliable twigs are made of it too.
It is sacred to underworld Juno, who is its patron,
And it is roofed in by a grove, where deep shadows mass
Along far wooded valleys. No one is ever permitted
To go down to earth's hidden places unless he has first
Plucked this golden-fledged growth out of its tree
And handed it over to fair Proserpina, to whom it belongs
By decree, her own special gift. And when it is plucked,
A second one always grows in its place, golden again,
And the foliage growing on it has the same metal sheen.
Therefore look up and search deep and when you have found i
Take hold of it boldly and duly. If fate has called you,
The bough will come away easily, of its own accord.
Otherwise, no matter how much strength you muster, you
    never will
Manage to quell it or cut it down with the toughest of blades.'

PART I

The Journey Back

Larkin's shade surprised me. He quoted Dante:

'Daylight was going and the umber air
Soothing every creature on the earth,
Freeing them from their labours everywhere.

I alone was girding myself to face
The ordeal of my journey and my duty
And not a thing had changed. as rush-hour buses

Bore the drained and laden through the city.
I might have been a wise king setting out
Under the Christmas lights – except that

It felt more like the forewarned journey back
Into the heartland of the ordinary.
Still my old self. Ready to knock one back.

A nine-to-five man who had seen poetry.'

Markings

I

We marked the pitch: four jackets for four goalposts,
That was all. The corners and the squares
Were there like longitude and latitude
Under the bumpy thistly ground, to be
Agreed about or disagreed about
When the time came. And then we picked the teams
And crossed the line our called names drew between us.

Youngsters shouting their heads off in a field
As the light died and they kept on playing
Because by then they were playing in their heads
And the actual kicked ball came to them
Like a dream heaviness, and their own hard
Breathing in the dark and skids on grass
Sounded like effort in another world...
It was quick and constant, a game that never need
Be played out. Some limit had been passed,
There was fleetness, furtherance, untiredness
In time that was extra, unforeseen and free.

II

You also loved lines pegged out in the garden,
The spade nicking the first straight edge along
The tight white string. Or string stretched perfectly
To mark the outline of a house foundation,
Pale timber battens set at right angles
For every corner, each freshly sawn new board
Spick and span in the oddly passive grass.
Or the imaginary line straight down
A field of grazing, to be ploughed open
From the rod stuck in one headrig to the rod
Stuck in the other.

III

All these things entered you
As if they were both the door and what came through it.
They marked the spot, marked time and held it open.
A mower parted the bronze sea of corn.
A windlass hauled the centre out of water.
Two men with a cross-cut kept it swimming
Into a felled beech backwards and forwards
So that they seemed to row the steady earth.

Three Drawings

1   *The Point*

Those were the days –
booting a leather football
truer and farther
than you ever expected!

It went rattling
hard and fast
over daisies and benweeds,
it thumped

but it sang too,
a kind of dry, ringing
foreclosure of sound.
Or else, a great catch

and a cry from the touch-line
to *Point her!* That spring
and unhampered smash-through!
Was it you

or the ball that kept going
beyond you, amazingly
higher and higher
and ruefully free?

2 *The Pulse*

The effortlessness
of a spinning reel. One quick
flick of the wrist
and your minnow sped away

whispering and silky
and nimbly laden.
It seemed to be all rise
and shine, the very opposite

of uphill going – it was pure
duration, and when it ended,
the pulse of the cast line
entering water

was smaller in your hand
than the remembered heartbeat
of a bird. Then, after all of that
runaway give, you were glad

when you reeled in and found
yourself strung, heel-tip
to rod-tip, into the river's
steady purchase and thrum.

3   *A Haul*

The one that got away
from Thor and the giant Hymer
was the world-serpent itself.
The god had baited his line

with an ox-head, spun it high
and plunged it into the depths.
But the big haul came to an end
when Thor's foot went through the boards

and Hymer panicked and cut
the line with a bait-knife. Then
roll-over, turmoil, whiplash!
A Milky Way in the water.

The hole he smashed in the boat
opened, the way Thor's head
opened out there on the sea.
He felt at one with space,

unroofed and obvious –
surprised in his empty arms
like some fabulous high-catcher
coming down without the ball.

Casting and Gathering

for Ted Hughes

Years and years ago, these sounds took sides:

On the left bank, a green silk tapered cast
Went whispering through the air, saying *hush*
And *lush*. entirely free, no matter whether
It swished above the hayfield or the river.

On the right bank, like a speeded-up corncrake,
A sharp ratcheting went on and on
Cutting across the stillness as another
Fisherman gathered line-lengths off his reel.

I am still standing there, awake and dreamy,
I have grown older and can see them both
Moving their arms and rods, working away,
Each one absorbed, proofed by the sounds he's making.

One sound is saying, 'You are not worth tuppence,
But neither is anybody. Watch it! Be severe.'
The other says, 'Go with it! Give and swerve.
You are everything you feel beside the river.'

I love hushed air. I trust contrariness.
Years and years go past and I do not move
For I see that when one man casts, the other gathers
And then *vice versa*, without changing sides.

Man and Boy

I

'Catch the old one first,'
(My father's joke was also old, and heavy
And predictable.) 'Then the young ones
Will all follow, and Bob's your uncle.'

On slow bright river evenings, the sweet time
Made him afraid we'd take too much for granted
And so our spirits must be lightly checked.

Blessed be down-to-earth! Blessed be highs!
Blessed be the detachment of dumb love
In that broad-backed, low-set man
Who feared debt all his life, but now and then
Could make a splash like the salmon he said was
'As big as a wee pork pig by the sound of it'.

II

In earshot of the pool where the salmon jumped
Back through its own unheard concentric soundwaves
A mower leans forever on his scythe.

He has mown himself to the centre of the field
And stands in a final perfect ring
Of sunlit stubble.

'Go and tell your father,' the mower says
(He said it to my father who told me)
'I have it mowed as clean as a new sixpence.'

My father is a barefoot boy with news,
Running at eye-level with weeds and stooks
On the afternoon of his own father's death.

The open, black half of the half-door waits.
I feel much heat and hurry in the air.
I feel his legs and quick heels far away

And strange as my own – when he will piggyback me
At a great height, light-headed and thin-boned,
Like a witless elder rescued from the fire.

Seeing Things

I

Inishbofin on a Sunday morning.
Sunlight, turfsmoke, seagulls, boatslip, diesel.
One by one we were being handed down
Into a boat that dipped and shilly-shallied
Scaresomely every time. We sat tight
On short cross-benches, in nervous twos and threes,
Obedient, newly close, nobody speaking
Except the boatmen, as the gunwales sank
And seemed they might ship water any minute.
The sea was very calm but even so,
When the engine kicked and our ferryman
Swayed for balance, reaching for the tiller,
I panicked at the shiftiness and heft
Of the craft itself. What guaranteed us –
That quick response and buoyancy and swim –
Kept me in agony. All the time
As we went sailing evenly across
The deep, still, seeable-down-into water,
It was as if I looked from another boat
Sailing through air, far up, and could see
How riskily we fared into the morning,
And loved in vain our bare, bowed, numbered heads.

II

Claritas. The dry-eyed Latin word
Is perfect for the carved stone of the water
Where Jesus stands up to his unwet knees
And John the Baptist pours out more water
Over his head: all this in bright sunlight
On the façade of a cathedral. Lines
Hard and thin and sinuous represent
The flowing river. Down between the lines
Little antic fish are all go. Nothing else.
And yet in that utter visibility
The stone's alive with what's invisible:
Waterweed, stirred sand-grains hurrying off,
The shadowy, unshadowed stream itself.
All afternoon, heat wavered on the steps
And the air we stood up to our eyes in wavered
Like the zig-zag hieroglyph for life itself.

Once upon a time my undrowned father
Walked into our yard. He had gone to spray
Potatoes in a field on the riverbank
And wouldn't bring me with him. The horse-sprayer
Was too big and new-fangled, bluestone might
Burn me in the eyes, the horse was fresh, I
Might scare the horse, and so on. I threw stones
At a bird on the shed roof, as much for
The clatter of the stones as anything,
But when he came back, I was inside the house
And saw him out the window, scatter-eyed
And daunted, strange without his hat,
His step unguided, his ghosthood immanent.
When he was turning on the riverbank,
The horse had rusted and reared up and pitched
Cart and sprayer and everything off balance
So the whole rig went over into a deep
Whirlpool, hoofs, chains, shafts, cartwheels, barrel
And tackle, all tumbling off the world,
And the hat already merrily swept along
The quieter reaches. That afternoon
I saw him face to face, he came to me
With his damp footprints out of the river,
And there was nothing between us there
That might not still be happily ever after.

The Ash Plant

He'll never rise again but he is ready.
Entered like a mirror by the morning,
He stares out the big window, wondering,
Not caring if the day is bright or cloudy.

An upstairs outlook on the whole country.
First milk-lorries, first smoke, cattle, trees
In damp opulence above damp hedges –
He has it to himself, he is like a sentry

Forgotten and unable to remember
The whys and wherefores of his lofty station,
Wakening relieved yet in position,
Disencumbered as a breaking comber.

As his head goes light with light, his wasting hand
Gropes desperately and finds the phantom limb
Of an ash plant in his grasp, which steadies him.
Now he has found his touch he can stand his ground

Or wield the stick like a silver bough and come
Walking again among us: the quoted judge.
I could have cut a better man out of the hedge!
God might have said the same, remembering Adam.

1. 1. 87

Dangerous pavements.
But I face the ice this year
With my father's stick.

An August Night

His hands were warm and small and knowledgeable.
When I saw them again last night, they were two ferrets,
Playing all by themselves in a moonlit field.

Field of Vision

I remember this woman who sat for years
In a wheelchair, looking straight ahead
Out the window at sycamore trees unleafing
And leafing at the far end of the lane.

Straight out past the TV in the corner,
The stunted, agitated hawthorn bush,
The same small calves with their backs to wind and rain,
The same acre of ragwort, the same mountain.

She was steadfast as the big window itself.
Her brow was clear as the chrome bits of the chair.
She never lamented once and she never
Carried a spare ounce of emotional weight.

Face to face with her was an education
Of the sort you got across a well-braced gate –
One of those lean, clean, iron, roadside ones
Between two whitewashed pillars, where you could see

Deeper into the country than you expected
And discovered that the field behind the hedge
Grew more distinctly strange as you kept standing
Focused and drawn in by what barred the way.

The Pitchfork

Of all implements, the pitchfork was the one
That came near to an imagined perfection:
When he tightened his raised hand and aimed with it,
It felt like a javelin, accurate and light.

So whether he played the warrior or the athlete
Or worked in earnest in the chaff and sweat,
He loved its grain of tapering, dark-flecked ash
Grown satiny from its own natural polish.

Riveted steel, turned timber, burnish, grain,
Smoothness, straightness, roundness, length and sheen.
Sweat-cured, sharpened, balanced, tested, fitted.
The springiness, the clip and dart of it.

And then when he thought of probes that reached the farthest,
He would see the shaft of a pitchfork sailing past
Evenly, imperturbably through space,
Its prongs starlit and absolutely soundless –

But has learned at last to follow that simple lead
Past its own aim, out to an other side
Where perfection – or nearness to it – is imagined
Not in the aiming but the opening hand.

A Basket of Chestnuts

There's a shadow-boost, a giddy strange assistance
That happens when you swing a loaded basket.
The lightness of the thing seems to diminish
The actual weight of what's being hoisted in it.

For a split second your hands feel unburdened,
Outstripped, dismayed, passed through.
Then just as unexpectedly comes rebound –
Downthrust and comeback ratifying you.

I recollect this basket full of chestnuts,
A really solid gather-up, all drag
And lustre, opulent and gravid
And golden-bowelled as a moneybag.

And I wish they could be painted, known for what
Pigment might see beyond them, what the reach
Of sense despairs of as it fails to reach it,
Especially the thwarted sense of touch.

Since Edward Maguire visited our house
In the autumn of 1973,
A basketful of chestnuts shines between us,
One that he did not paint when he painted me –

Although it was what he thought he'd maybe use
As a decoy or a coffer for the light
He captured in the toecaps of my shoes.
But it wasn't in the picture and is not.

What's there is comeback, especially for him.
In oils and brushwork we are ratified.
And the basket shines and foxfire chestnuts gleam
Where he passed through, unburdened and dismayed.

The Biretta

Like Gaul, the biretta was divided
Into three parts: triple-finned black serge,
A shipshape pillbox, its every slope and edge
Trimly articulated and decided.

Its insides were crimped satin; it was heavy too
But sported a light flossy tassel
That the backs of my fingers remember well,
And it left a dark red line on the priest's brow.

I received it into my hand from the hand
Of whoever was celebrant, one thin
Fastidious movement up and out and in
In the name of the Father and of the Son AND

Of the Holy Ghost ... I placed it on the steps
Where it seemed to batten down, even half-resist
All of the brisk proceedings of the Mass –
The chalice drunk off and the patted lips.

The first time I saw one, I heard a shout
As an El Greco ascetic rose before me
Preaching hellfire, Saurian and stormy,
Adze-head on the rampage in the pulpit.

Sanctuaries. Marble. Kneeling boards. Vocation.
Some it made look squashed, some clean and tall.
It was antique as armour in a hall
And put the wind up me and my generation.

Now I turn it upside down and it is a boat –
A paper boat, or the one that wafts into
The first lines of the *Purgatorio*
As poetry lifts its eyes and clears its throat.

Or maybe that small boat out of the bronze age
Where the oars are needles and the worked gold frail
As the intact half of a hatched-out shell,
Refined beyond the dross into sheer image.

But in the end it's as likely to be the one
In Matthew Lawless's painting, *The Sick Call*,
Where the scene is out on a river and it's all
Solid, pathetic and Irish Victorian.

In which case, however, his reverence wears a hat.
Undaunting, half domestic, loved in crises,
He sits listening as each long oar dips and rises,
Sad for his worthy life and fit for it.

The Settle Bed

Willed down, waited for, in place at last and for good.
Trunk-hasped, cart-heavy, painted an ignorant brown.
And pew-strait, bin-deep, standing four-square as an ark.

If I lie in it, I am cribbed in seasoned deal
Dry as the unkindled boards of a funeral ship.
My measure has been taken, my ear shuttered up.

Yet I hear an old sombre tide awash in the headboard:
Unpathetic *och ochs* and *och hohs*, the long bedtime
Anthems of Ulster, unwilling, unbeaten,

Protestant, Catholic, the Bible, the beads,
Long talks at gables by moonlight, boots on the hearth,
The small hours chimed sweetly away so next thing it was

The cock on the ridge-tiles.
                        And now this is 'an inheritance' –
Upright, rudimentary, unshiftably planked
In the long ago, yet willable forward

Again and again and again, cargoed with
Its own dumb, tongue-and-groove worthiness
And un-get-roundable weight. But to conquer that weight,

Imagine a dower of settle beds tumbled from heaven
Like some nonsensical vengeance come on the people,
Then learn from that harmless barrage that whatever
  is given

Can always be reimagined, however four-square,
Plank-thick, hull-stupid and out of its time
It happens to be. You are free as the lookout,

That far-seeing joker posted high over the fog,
Who declared by the time that he had got himself down
The actual ship had been stolen away from beneath him.

The Schoolbag

in memoriam John Hewitt

My handsewn leather schoolbag. Forty years.
Poet, you were *nel mezzo del cammin*
When I shouldered it, half-full of blue-lined jotters,
And saw the classroom charts, the displayed bean,

The wallmap with its spray of shipping lanes
Describing arcs across the blue North Channel...
And in the middle of the road to school,
Ox-eye daisies and wild dandelions.

Learning's easy carried! The bag is light,
Scuffed and supple and unemptiable
As an itinerant school conjuror's hat.
So take it, for a word-hoard and a handsel,

As you step out trig and look back all at once
Like a child on his first morning leaving parents.

Glanmore Revisited

1 *Scrabble*
in memoriam Tom Delaney, archaeologist

Bare flags. Pump water. Winter-evening cold.
Our backs might never warm up but our faces
Burned from the hearth-blaze and the hot whiskeys.
It felt remembered even then, an old
Rightness half-imagined or foretold,
As green sticks hissed and spat into the ashes
And whatever rampaged out there couldn't reach us,
Firelit, shuttered, slated and stone-walled.

Year after year, our game of Scrabble: love
Taken for granted like any other word
That was chanced on and allowed within the rules.
So 'scrabble' let it be. Intransitive.
Meaning to scratch or rake at something hard.
Which is what he hears. Our scraping, clinking tools.

2   *The Cot*

Scythe and axe and hedge-clippers, the shriek
Of the gate the children used to swing on,
Poker, scuttle, tongs, a gravel rake –
The old activity starts up again
But starts up differently. We're on our own
Years later in the same *locus amoenus*,
Tenants no longer, but in full possession
Of an emptied house and whatever keeps between us.

Which must be more than keepsakes, even though
The child's cot's back in place where Catherine
Woke in the dawn and answered *doodle doo*
To the rooster in the farm across the road –
And is the same cot I myself slept in
When the whole world was a farm that eked and crowed.

Only days after a friend had cut his name
Into the ash, our kids stripped off the bark –
The first time I was really angry at them.
I was flailing round the house like a man berserk
And maybe overdoing it, although
The business had moved me at the time;
It brought back those blood-brother scenes where two
Braves nick wrists and cross them for a sign.

Where it shone like bone exposed is healed up now.
The bark's thick-eared and welted with a scar –
Like the hero's in a recognition scene
In which old nurse sees old wound, then clasps brow
(Astonished at what all this starts to mean)
And tears surprise the veteran of the war.

4 *1973*

The corrugated iron growled like thunder
When March came in; then as the year turned warmer
And invalids and bulbs came up from under,
I hibernated on behind the dormer,
Staring through shaken branches at the hill,
Dissociated, like an ailing farmer
Chloroformed against things seasonal
In a reek of cigarette smoke and dropped ash.

Lent came in next, also like a lion
Sinewy and wild for discipline,
A fasted will marauding through the body;
And I taunted it with scents of nicotine
As I lit one off another, and felt rash,
And stirred in the deep litter of the study.

Breaking and entering: from early on,
Words that thrilled me far more than they scared me –
And still did, when I came into my own
Masquerade as a man of property.
Even then, my first impulse was never
To double-bar a door or lock a gate;
And fitted blinds and curtains drawn over
Seemed far too self-protective and uptight.

But I scared myself when I re-entered here,
My own first breaker-in, with an instruction
To saw up the old bed-frame, since the stair
Was much too narrow for it. A bad action,
So Greek with consequence, so dangerous,
Only pure words and deeds secure the house.

6 Bedside Reading

The whole place airier. Big summer trees
Stirring at eye level when we waken
And little shoots of ivy creeping in
Unless they've been trained out – like memories
You've trained so long now they can show their face
And keep their distance. White-mouthed depression
Swims out from its shadow like a dolphin
With wet, unreadable, unfurtive eyes.

I swim in Homer. In Book Twenty-three.
At last Odysseus and Penelope
Waken together. One bedpost of the bed
Is the living trunk of an old olive tree
And is their secret. As ours could have been ivy,
Evergreen, atremble and unsaid.

7 *The Skylight*

You were the one for skylights. I opposed
Cutting into the seasoned tongue-and-groove
Of pitch pine. I liked it low and closed,
Its claustrophobic, nest-up-in-the-roof
Effect. I liked the snuff-dry feeling,
The perfect, trunk-lid fit of the old ceiling.
Under there, it was all hutch and hatch.
The blue slates kept the heat like midnight thatch.

But when the slates came off, extravagant
Sky entered and held surprise wide open.
For days I felt like an inhabitant
Of that house where the man sick of the palsy
Was lowered through the roof, had his sins forgiven,
Was healed, took up his bed and walked away.

A Pillowed Head

Matutinal. Mother-of-pearl
Summer come early. Slashed carmines
And washed milky blues.

To be first on the road,
Up with the ground-mists and pheasants.
To be older and grateful

That this time you too were half-grateful
The pangs had begun – prepared
And clear-headed, foreknowing

The trauma, entering on it
With full consent of the will.
(The first time, dismayed and arrayed

In your cut-off white cotton gown,
You were more bride than earth-mother
Up on the stirrup-rigged bed,

Who were self-possessed now
To the point of a walk on the pier
Before you checked in.)

And then later on I half-fainted
When the little slapped palpable girl
Was handed to me; but as usual

Came to in two wide-open eyes
That had been dawned into farther
Than ever, and had outseen the last

Of all those mornings of waiting
When your domed brow was one long held silence
And the dawn chorus anything but.

A Royal Prospect

On the day of their excursion up the Thames
To Hampton Court, they were nearly sunstruck.
She with her neck bared in a page-boy cut,
He all dreamy anyhow, wild for her
But pretending to be a thousand miles away,
Studying the boat's wake in the water.
And here are the photographs. Head to one side,
In her sleeveless blouse, one bare shoulder high
And one arm loose, a bird with a dropped wing
Surprised in cover. He looks at you straight,
Assailable, enamoured, full of vows,
Young dauphin in the once-upon-a-time.
And next the lowish red-brick Tudor frontage.
No more photographs, however, now
We are present there as the smell of grass
And suntan oil, standing like their sixth sense
Behind them at the entrance to the maze,
Heartbroken for no reason, willing them
To dare it to the centre they are lost for...
Instead, like reflections staggered through warped glass,
They reappear as in a black and white
Old grainy newsreel, where their pleasure-boat
Goes back spotlit across sunken bridges
And they alone are borne downstream unscathed,
Between mud banks where the wounded rave all night
At flameless blasts and echoless gunfire –
In all of which is ominously figured
Their free passage through historic times,
Like a silk train being brushed across a leper
Or the safe conduct of two royal favourites,
Unhindered and resented and bright-eyed.
So let them keep a tally of themselves
And be accountable when called upon
For although by every golden mean their lot

Is fair and due, pleas will be allowed
Against every right and title vested in them
(And in a court where mere innocuousness
Has never gained approval or acquittal.)

A Retrospect

I

The whole county apparently afloat:
Every road bridging or skirting water,
The land islanded, the field drains still as moats.

A bulrush sentried the lough shore: I had to
Wade barefoot over spongy, ice-cold marsh
(Soft bottom with bog water seeping through

The netted weeds) to get near where it stood
Perennially anomalous and dry,
Like chalk or velvet rooting in the mud.

Everything ran into water-colour.
The skyline was full up to the lip
As if the earth were going to brim over,

As if we moved in the first stealth of flood
For remember, at one place, the swim and flow
From hidden springs made a river in the road.

II

Another trip they seemed to keep repeating
Was up to Glenshane Pass – his 'Trail of Tears',
As he'd say every time, and point out streams
He first saw on the road to boarding school.
And then he'd quote Sir John Davies' dispatch
About his progress through there from Dungannon
With Chichester in 1608:
'The wild inhabitants wondered as much
To see the King's deputy, as Virgil's ghosts
Wondered to see Aeneas alive in Hell.'

They liked the feel of the valley out behind,
As if a ladder leaned against the world
And they were climbing it but might fall back
Into the total air and emptiness
They carried on their shoulders.

                    The old road
Went up and up, it was lover country,
Their drive-in in the sky, where each parked car
Played possum in the twilight and clouds moved
Smokily in the deep of polished roofs
And dormant windscreens.

                    And there they were,
Astray in the hill-fort of all pleasures
Where air was other breath and grass a whisper,
Feeling empowered but still somehow constrained:
Young marrieds, used now to the licit within doors,
They fell short of the sweetness that had lured them.
No nest in rushes, the heather bells unbruised,
The love-drink of the mountain streams untasted.

So when they turned, they turned with the fasted eyes
Of wild inhabitants, and parked in silence
A bit down from the summit, where the brae
Swept off like a balcony, then seemed to drop
Sheer towards the baronies and cantreds.
Evening was dam water they saw down through.
The scene stood open, the visit lasted,
They gazed beyond themselves until he eased
The brake off and they freewheeled quickly
Before going into gear, with all their usual old
High-pitched strain and gradual declension.

The Rescue

In drifts of sleep I came upon you
Buried to your waist in snow.
You reached your arms out: I came to
Like water in a dream of thaw.

Wheels within Wheels

I

The first real grip I ever got on things
Was when I learned the art of pedalling
(By hand) a bike turned upside down, and drove
Its back wheel preternaturally fast.
I loved the disappearance of the spokes,
The way the space between the hub and rim
Hummed with transparency. If you threw
A potato into it, the hooped air
Spun mush and drizzle back into your face;
If you touched it with a straw, the straw frittered.
Something about the way those pedal treads
Worked very palpably at first against you
And then began to sweep your hand ahead
Into a new momentum – that all entered me
Like an access of free power, as if belief
Caught up and spun the objects of belief
In an orbit coterminous with longing.

II

But enough was not enough. Who ever saw
The limit in the given anyhow?
In fields beyond our house there was a well
('The well' we called it. It was more a hole
With water in it, with small hawthorn trees
On one side, and a muddy, dungy ooze
On the other, all tramped through by cattle).
I loved that too. I loved the turbid smell,
The sump-life of the place like old chain oil.
And there, next thing, I brought my bicycle.
I stood its saddle and its handlebars
Into the soft bottom, I touched the tyres
To the water's surface, then turned the pedals

Until like a mill-wheel pouring at the treadles
(But here reversed and lashing a mare's tail)
The world-refreshing and immersed back wheel
Spun lace and dirt-suds there before my eyes
And showered me in my own regenerate clays.
For weeks I made a nimbus of old glit.
Then the hub jammed, rims rusted, the chain snapped.

III

Nothing rose to the occasion after that
Until, in a circus ring, drumrolled and spotlit,
Cowgirls wheeled in, each one immaculate
At the still centre of a lariat.
Perpetuum mobile. Sheer pirouette.
Tumblers. Jongleurs. Ring-a-rosies. *Stet!*

The Sounds of Rain

in memoriam Richard Ellmann

I

An all-night drubbing overflow on boards
On the verandah. I dwelt without thinking
In the long moil of it, and then came to
To dripping eaves and light, saying into myself
Proven, weightless sayings of the dead.
Things like *He'll be missed* and *You'll have to thole.*

II

It could have been the drenched weedy gardens
Of Peredelkino: a reverie
Of looking out from late-winter gloom
Lit by tangerines and the clear of vodka,
Where Pasternak, lenient yet austere,
Answered for himself without insistence.

'I had the feeling of an immense debt,'
He said (it is recorded). 'So many years
Just writing lyric poetry and translating.
I felt there was some duty...Time was passing.
And with all its faults, it has more value
Than those early... It is richer, more humane.'

Or it could have been the thaw and puddles
Of Athens Street where William Alfred stood
On the wet doorstep, remembering the friend
Who died at sixty. 'After "Summer Tides"
There would have been a deepening, you know,
Something ampler... Ah well. Good-night again.'

III

The eaves a water-fringe and steady lash
Of summer downpour: *You are steeped in luck,*
I hear them say, *Steeped, steeped, steeped in luck.*
And hear the flood too, gathering from under,
Biding and boding like a masterwork
Or a named name that overbrims itself.

Fosterling

'That heavy greenness fostered by water'

At school I loved one picture's heavy greenness –
Horizons rigged with windmills' arms and sails.
The millhouses' still outlines. Their in-placeness
Still more in place when mirrored in canals.
I can't remember never having known
The immanent hydraulics of a land
Of *glar* and *glit* and floods at *dailigone*.
My silting hope. My lowlands of the mind.

Heaviness of being. And poetry
Sluggish in the doldrums of what happens.
Me waiting until I was nearly fifty
To credit marvels. Like the tree-clock of tin cans
The tinkers made. So long for air to brighten,
Time to be dazzled and the heart to lighten.

PART II

SQUARINGS

1 Lightenings

i

Shifting brilliancies. Then winter light
In a doorway, and on the stone doorstep
A beggar shivering in silhouette.

So the particular judgement might be set:
Bare wallstead and a cold hearth rained into –
Bright puddle where the soul-free cloud-life roams.

And after the commanded journey, what?
Nothing magnificent, nothing unknown.
A gazing out from far away, alone.

And it is not particular at all,
Just old truth dawning: there is no next-time-round.
Unroofed scope. Knowledge-freshening wind.

ii

Roof it again. Batten down. Dig in.
Drink out of tin. Know the scullery cold,
A latch, a door-bar, forged tongs and a grate.

Touch the cross-beam, drive iron in a wall,
Hang a line to verify the plumb
From lintel, coping-stone and chimney-breast.

Relocate the bedrock in the threshold.
Take squarings from the recessed gable pane.
Make your study the unregarded floor.

Sink every impulse like a bolt. Secure
The bastion of sensation. Do not waver
Into language. Do not waver in it.

iii

Squarings? In the game of marbles, squarings
Were all those anglings, aimings, feints and squints
You were allowed before you'd shoot, all those

Hunkerings, tensings, pressures of the thumb,
Test-outs and pull-backs, re-envisagings,
All the ways your arms kept hoping towards

Blind certainties that were going to prevail
Beyond the one-off moment of the pitch.
A million million accuracies passed

Between your muscles' outreach and that space
Marked with three round holes and a drawn line.
You squinted out from a skylight of the world.

iv

Beneath the ocean of itself, the crowd
In Roman theatres could hear another
Stronger groundswell coming through.

It was like the steady message in a shell
Held to the ear in earshot of the sea:
Words being spoken on the scene arrived

Resonating up through the walls of urns.
The cordoned air rolled back, wave upon wave
Of classic mouthfuls amplified and faded.

How airy and how earthed it felt up there,
Bare to the world, light-headed, volatile
And carried like the rests in tides or music.

v

Three marble holes thumbed in the concrete road
Before the concrete hardened still remained
Three decades after the marble-player vanished

Into Australia. Three stops to play
The music of the arbitrary on.
Blow on them now and hear an undersong

Your levelled breath made once going over
The empty bottle. Improvise. Make free
Like old hay in its flimsy afterlife

High on a windblown hedge. Ocarina earth.
Three listening posts up on some hard-baked tier
Above the resonating amphorae.

vi

Once, as a child, out in a field of sheep,
Thomas Hardy pretended to be dead
And lay down flat among their dainty shins.

In that sniffed-at, bleated-into, grassy space
He experimented with infinity.
His small cool brow was like an anvil waiting

For sky to make it sing the perfect pitch
Of his dumb being, and that stir he caused
In the fleece-hustle was the original

Of a ripple that would travel eighty years
Outward from there, to be the same ripple
Inside him at its last circumference.

(I misremembered. He went down on all fours,
Florence Emily says, crossing a ewe-leaze.
Hardy sought the creatures face to face,

Their witless eyes and liability
To panic made him feel less alone,
Made proleptic sorrow stand a moment

Over him, perfectly known and sure.
And then the flock's dismay went swimming on
Into the blinks and murmurs and deflections

He'd know at parties in renowned old age
When sometimes he imagined himself a ghost
And circulated with that new perspective.)

viii

The annals say: when the monks of Clonmacnoise
Were all at prayers inside the oratory
A ship appeared above them in the air.

The anchor dragged along behind so deep
It hooked itself into the altar rails
And then, as the big hull rocked to a standstill,

A crewman shinned and grappled down the rope
And struggled to release it. But in vain.
'This man can't bear our life here and will drown,'

The abbot said, 'unless we help him.' So
They did, the freed ship sailed, and the man climbed back
Out of the marvellous as he had known it.

ix

A boat that did not rock or wobble once
Sat in long grass one Sunday afternoon
In nineteen forty-one or two. The heat

Out on Lough Neagh and in where cattle stood
Jostling and skittering near the hedge
Grew redolent of the tweed skirt and tweed sleeve

I nursed on. I remember little treble
Timber-notes their smart heels struck from planks,
Me cradled in an elbow like a secret

Open now as the eye of heaven was then
Above three sisters talking, talking steady
In a boat the ground still falls and falls from under.

x

Overhang of grass and seedling birch
On the quarry face. Rock-hob where you watched
All that cargoed brightness travelling

Above and beyond and sumptuously across
The water in its clear deep dangerous holes
On the quarry floor. Ultimate

Fathomableness, ultimate
Stony up-againstness: could you reconcile
What was diaphanous there with what was massive?

Were you equal to or were you opposite
To build-ups so promiscuous and weightless?
Shield your eyes, look up and face the music.

xi

To put a glass roof on the handball alley
Where a hopped ball cut merciless angles
In and out of play, or levelled true

For the unanswerable dead-root...
He alone, our walking weathercock,
Our peeled eye at the easel, had the right

To make a studio of that free maze,
To turn light outside in and curb the space
Where accident got tricked to accuracy

And rain was rainier for being blown
Across the grid and texture of the concrete.
He scales the world at arm's length, gives thumbs up.

And lightening? One meaning of that
Beyond the usual sense of alleviation,
Illumination, and so on, is this:

A phenomenal instant when the spirit flares
With pure exhilaration before death –
The good thief in us harking to the promise!

So paint him on Christ's right hand, on a promontory
Scanning empty space, so body-racked he seems
Untranslatable into the bliss

Ached for at the moon-rim of his forehead,
By nail-craters on the dark side of his brain:
This day thou shalt be with Me in Paradise.

2 Settings

xiii

Hazel stealth. A trickle in the culvert.
Athletic sealight on the doorstep slab,
On the sea itself, on silent roofs and gables.

Whitewashed suntraps. Hedges hot as chimneys.
Chairs on all fours. A plate-rack braced and laden.
The fossil poetry of hob and slate.

Desire within its moat, dozing at ease –
Like a gorged cormorant on the rock at noon,
Exiled and in tune with the big glitter.

Re-enter this as the adult of solitude,
The silence-forder and the definite
Presence you sensed withdrawing first time round.

xiv

One afternoon I was seraph on gold leaf.
I stood on the railway sleepers hearing larks,
Grasshoppers, cuckoos, dogbarks, trainer planes

Cutting and modulating and drawing off.
Heat wavered on the immaculate line
And shine of the cogged rails. On either side,

Dog daisies stood like vestals, the hot stones
Were clover-meshed and streaked with engine oil.
Air spanned, passage waited, the balance rode,

Nothing prevailed, whatever was in store
Witnessed itself already taking place
In a time marked by assent and by hiatus.

And strike this scene in gold too, in relief,
So that a greedy eye cannot exhaust it:
Stable straw, Rembrandt-gleam and burnish

Where my father bends to a tea-chest packed with salt,
The hurricane lamp held up at eye-level
In his bunched left fist, his right hand foraging

For the unbleeding, vivid-fleshed bacon,
Home-cured hocks pulled up into the light
For pondering a while and putting back.

That night I owned the piled grain of Egypt.
I watched the sentry's torchlight on the hoard.
I stood in the door, unseen and blazed upon.

xvi

Rat-poison the colour of blood pudding
Went phosphorescent when it was being spread:
Its sparky rancid shine under the blade

Brought everything to life – like news of murder
Or the sight of a parked car occupied by lovers
On a side road, or stories of bull victims.

If a muse had sung the anger of Achilles
It would not have heightened the world-danger more.
It was all there in the fresh rat-poison

Corposant on mouldy, dried-up crusts.
On winter evenings I loved its reek and risk.
And windfalls freezing on the outhouse roof.

What were the virtues of an eelskin? What
Was the eel itself? A rib of water drawn
Out of the water, an ell yielded up

From glooms and whorls and slatings,
Rediscovered once it had been skinned.
When a wrist was bound with eelskin, energy

Redounded in that arm, a waterwheel
Turned in the shoulder, mill-races poured
And made your elbow giddy.

Your hand felt unconstrained and spirited
As heads and tails that wriggled in the mud
Aristotle supposed all eels were sprung from.

xviii

Like a foul-mouthed god of hemp come down to rut,
The rope-man stumped about and praised new rope
With talk of how thick it was, or how long and strong,

And how you could take it into your own hand
And feel it. His perfect, tight-bound wares
Made a circle round him: the makings of reins

And belly-bands and halters. And of slippage –
For even then, knee-high among the farmers,
I knew the rope-man menaced them with freedoms

They were going to turn their backs on; and knew too
His powerlessness once the fair-hill emptied
And he had to break the circle and start loading.

xix

Memory as a building or a city,
Well lighted, well laid out, appointed with
Tableaux vivants and costumed effigies –

Statues in purple cloaks, or painted red,
Ones wearing crowns, ones smeared with mud or blood:
So that the mind's eye could haunt itself

With fixed associations and learn to read
Its own contents in meaningful order,
Ancient textbooks recommended that

Familiar places be linked deliberately
With a code of images. You knew the portent
In each setting, you blinked and concentrated.

On Red Square, the brick wall of the Kremlin
Looked unthreatening, in scale, just right for people
To behave well under, inside or outside.

The big cleared space in front was dizzying.
I looked across a heave and sweep of cobbles
Like the ones that beamed up in my dream of flying

Above the old cart road, with all the air
Fanning off beneath my neck and breastbone.
(The cloud-roamer, was it, Stalin called Pasternak?)

Terrible history and protected joys!
Plosive horse-dung on 1940s' roads.
The newsreel bomb-hits, as harmless as dust-puffs.

xxi

Once and only once I fired a gun –
A .22. At a square of handkerchief
Pinned on a tree about sixty yards away.

It exhilarated me – the bullet's song
So effortlessly at my fingertip,
The target's single shocking little jerk,

A whole new quickened sense of what *rifle* meant.
And then again as it was in the beginning
I saw the soul like a white cloth snatched away

Across dark galaxies and felt that shot
For the sin it was against eternal life –
Another phrase dilating in new light.

xxii

Where does spirit live? Inside or outside
Things remembered, made things, things unmade?
What came first, the seabird's cry or the soul

Imagined in the dawn cold when it cried?
Where does it roost at last? On dungy sticks
In a jackdaw's nest up in the old stone tower

Or a marble bust commanding the parterre?
How habitable is perfected form?
And how inhabited the windy light?

What's the use of a held note or held line
That cannot be assailed for reassurance?
(Set questions for the ghost of W.B.)

xxiii

On the bus-trip into saga country
Ivan Malinowski wrote a poem
About the nuclear submarines offshore

From an abandoned whaling station.
I remember it as a frisson, but cannot
Remember any words. What I wanted then

Was a poem of utter evening:
The thirteenth century, weird midnight sun
Setting at eye-level with Snorri Sturluson

Who has come out to bathe in a hot spring
And sit through the stillness after milking time,
Laved and ensconced in the throne-room of his mind.

Deserted harbour stillness. Every stone
Clarified and dormant under water,
The harbour wall a masonry of silence.

Fullness. Shimmer. Laden high Atlantic
The moorings barely stirred in, very slight
Clucking of the swell against boat boards.

Perfected vision: cockle minarets
Consigned down there with green-slicked bottle glass,
Shell-debris and a reddened bud of sandstone.

Air and ocean known as antecedents
Of each other. In apposition with
Omnipresence, equilibrium, brim.

3 Crossings

xxv

Travelling south at dawn, going full out
Through high-up stone-wall country, the rocks still cold,
Rainwater gleaming here and there ahead,

I took a turn and met the fox stock-still,
Face-to-face in the middle of the road.
Wildness tore through me as he dipped and wheeled

In a level-running tawny breakaway.
O neat head, fabled brush and astonished eye
My blue Volkswagen flared into with morning!

Let rebirth come through water, through desire,
Through crawling backwards across clinic floors:
I have to cross back through that startled iris.

xxvi

Only to come up, year after year, behind
Those open-ended, canvas-covered trucks
Full of soldiers sitting cramped and staunch,

Their hands round gun-barrels, their gaze abroad
In dreams out of the body-heated metal.
Silent, time-proofed, keeping an even distance

Beyond the windscreen glass, carried ahead
On the phantasmal flow-back of the road,
They still mean business in the here and now.

So draw no attention, steer and concentrate
On the space that flees between like a speeded-up
Meltdown of souls from the straw-flecked ice of hell.

xxvii

Everything flows. Even a solid man,
A pillar to himself and to his trade,
All yellow boots and stick and soft felt hat,

Can sprout wings at the ankle and grow fleet
As the god of fair days, stone posts, roads and crossroads,
Guardian of travellers and psychopomp.

'Look for a man with an ashplant on the boat,'
My father told his sister setting out
For London, 'and stay near him all night

And you'll be safe.' Flow on, flow on
The journey of the soul with its soul guide
And the mysteries of dealing-men with sticks!

xxviii

The ice was like a bottle. We lined up
Eager to re-enter the long slide
We were bringing to perfection, time after time

Running and readying and letting go
Into a sheerness that was its own reward:
A farewell to surefootedness, a pitch

Beyond our usual hold upon ourselves.
And what went on kept going, from grip to give,
The narrow milky way in the black ice,

The race-up, the free passage and return –
It followed on itself like a ring of light
We knew we'd come through and kept sailing towards.

xxix

Scissor-and-slap abruptness of a latch.
Its coldness to the thumb. Its see-saw lift
And drop and innocent harshness.

Which is a music of binding and of loosing
Unheard in this generation, but there to be
Called up or called down at a touch renewed.

Once the latch pronounces, roof
Is original again, threshold fatal,
The sanction powerful as the foreboding.

Your footstep is already known, so bow
Just a little, raise your right hand,
Make impulse one with wilfulness, and enter.

xxx

On St Brigid's Day the new life could be entered
By going through her girdle of straw rope:
The proper way for men was right leg first,

Then right arm and right shoulder, head, then left
Shoulder, arm and leg. Women drew it down
Over the body and stepped out of it.

The open they came into by these moves
Stood opener, hoops came off the world,
They could feel the February air

Still soft above their heads and imagine
The limp rope fray and flare like wind-borne gleanings
Or an unhindered goldfinch over ploughland.

xxxi

Not an avenue and not a bower.
For a quarter-mile or so, where the county road
Is running straight across North Antrim bog,

Tall old fir trees line it on both sides.
Scotch firs, that is. Calligraphic shocks
Bushed and tufted in prevailing winds.

You drive into a meaning made of trees.
Or not exactly trees. It is a sense
Of running through and under without let,

Of glimpse and dapple. A life all trace and skim
The car has vanished out of. A fanned nape
Sensitive to the millionth of a flicker.

xxxii

Running water never disappointed.
Crossing water always furthered something.
Stepping stones were stations of the soul.

A kesh could mean the track some called a *causey*
Raised above the wetness of the bog,
Or the causey where it bridged old drains and streams.

It steadies me to tell these things. Also
I cannot mention keshes or the ford
Without my father's shade appearing to me

On a path towards sunset, eyeing spades and clothes
That turf cutters stowed perhaps or souls cast off
Before they crossed the log that spans the burn.

xxxiii

Be literal a moment. Recollect
Walking out on what had been emptied out
After he died, turning your back and leaving.

That morning tiles were harder, windows colder,
The raindrops on the pane more scourged, the grass
Barer to the sky, more wind-harrowed,

Or so it seemed. The house that he had planned
'Plain, big, straight, ordinary, you know,'
A paradigm of rigour and correction,

Rebuke to fanciness and shrine to limit,
Stood firmer than ever for its own idea
Like a printed X-ray for the X-rayed body.

xxxiv

Yeats said, *To those who see spirits, human skin*
For a long time afterwards appears most coarse.
The face I see that all falls short of since

Passes down an aisle: I share the bus
From San Francisco Airport into Berkeley
With one other passenger, who's dropped

At the Treasure Island military base
Half-way across Bay Bridge. Vietnam-bound,
He could have been one of the newly dead come back,

Unsurprisable but still disappointed,
Having to bear his farmboy self again,
His shaving cuts, his otherworldly brow.

xxxv

Shaving cuts. The pallor of bad habits.
Sunday afternoons, when summer idled
And couples walked the road along the Foyle,

We brought a shaving mirror to our window
In the top storey of the boarders' dorms:
Lovers in the happy valley, cars

Eager-backed and silent, the absolute river
Between us and it all. We tilted the glass up
Into the sun and found the range and shone

A flitting light on what we could not have.
Brightness played over them in chancy sweeps
Like flashes from a god's shield or a dance-floor.

xxxvi

And yes, my friend, we too walked through a valley.
Once. In darkness. With all the streetlamps off.
As danger gathered and the march dispersed.

Scene from Dante, made more memorable
By one of his head-clearing similes –
Fireflies, say, since the policemen's torches

Clustered and flicked and tempted us to trust
Their unpredictable, attractive light.
We were like herded shades who had to cross

And did cross, in a panic, to the car
Parked as we'd left it, that gave when we got in
Like Charon's boat under the faring poets.

4 Squarings

In famous poems by the sage Han Shan,
Cold Mountain is a place that can also mean
A state of mind. Or different states of mind

At different times, for the poems seem
One-off, impulsive, the kind of thing that starts
I have sat here facing the Cold Mountain

For twenty-nine years, or *There is no path*
That goes all the way – enviable stuff,
Unfussy and believable.

Talking about it isn't good enough
But quoting from it at least demonstrates
The virtue of an art that knows its mind.

We climbed the Capitol by moonlight, felt
The transports of temptation on the heights:
We were privileged and belated and we knew it.

Then something in me moved to prophesy
Against the beloved stand-offishness of marble
And all emulation of stone-cut verses.

'Down with form triumphant, long live,' (said I)
'Form mendicant and convalescent. We attend
The come-back of pure water and the prayer-wheel.'

To which a voice replied, 'Of course we do.
But the others are in the Forum Café waiting,
Wondering where we are. What'll you have?'

xxxix

When you sat, far-eyed and cold, in the basalt throne
Of 'the wishing chair' at Giant's Causeway,
The small of your back made very solid sense.

Like a papoose at sap-time strapped to a maple tree,
You gathered force out of the world-tree's hardness.
If you stretched your hand forth, things might turn to stone.

But you were only goose-fleshed skin and bone,
The rocks and wonder of the world were only
Lava crystallized, salts of the earth

The wishing chair gave a savour to, its kelp
And ozone freshening your outlook
Beyond the range you thought you'd settled for.

xl

I was four but I turned four hundred maybe
Encountering the ancient dampish feel
Of a clay floor. Maybe four thousand even.

Anyhow, there it was. Milk poured for cats
In a rank puddle-place, splash-darkened mould
Around the terracotta water-crock.

Ground of being. Body's deep obedience
To all its shifting tenses. A half-door
Opening directly into starlight.

Out of that earth house I inherited
A stack of singular, cold memory-weights
To load me, hand and foot, in the scale of things.

xli

Sand-bed, they said. And gravel-bed. Before
I knew river shallows or river pleasures
I knew the ore of longing in those words.

The places I go back to have not failed
But will not last. Waist-deep in cow-parsley,
I re-enter the swim, riding or quelling

The very currents memory is composed of,
Everything accumulated ever
As I took squarings from the tops of bridges

Or the banks of self at evening.
Lick of fear. Sweet transience. Flirt and splash.
Crumpled flow the sky-dipped willows trailed in.

xlii

Heather and kesh and turf stacks reappear
Summer by summer still, grasshoppers and all,
The same yet rarer: fields of the nearly blessed

Where gaunt ones in their shirtsleeves stooped and dug
Or stood alone at dusk surveying bog-banks –
Apparitions now, yet active still

And territorial, still sure of their ground,
Still interested, not knowing how far
The country of the shades has been pushed back,

How long the lark has stopped outside these fields
And only seems unstoppable to them
Caught like a far hill in a freak of sunshine.

xliii

Choose one set of tracks and track a hare
Until the prints stop, just like that, in snow.
End of the line. Smooth drifts. Where did she go?

Back on her tracks, of course, then took a spring
Yards off to the side; clean break; no scent or sign.
She landed in her form and ate the snow.

Consider too the ancient hieroglyph
Of 'hare and zig-zag', which meant 'to exist',
To be on the *qui vive*, weaving and dodging

Like our friend who sprang (goodbye) beyond our ken
And missed a round at last (but of course he'd stood it):
The shake-the-heart, the dew-hammer, the far-eyed.

xliv

All gone into the world of light? Perhaps
As we read the line sheer forms do crowd
The starry vestibule. Otherwise

They do not. What lucency survives
Is blanched as worms on nightlines I would lift,
Ungratified if always well prepared

For the nothing there – which was only what had been there.
Although in fact it is more like a caught line snapping,
That moment of admission of *All gone*,

When the rod butt loses touch and the tip drools
And eddies swirl a dead leaf past in silence
Swifter (it seems) than the water's passage.

For certain ones what was written may come true:
They shall live on in the distance
At the mouths of rivers.

For our ones, no. They will re-enter
Dryness that was heaven on earth to them,
Happy to eat the scones baked out of clay.

For some, perhaps, the delta's reed-beds
And cold bright-footed seabirds always wheeling.
For our ones, snuff

And hob-soot and the heat off ashes.
And a judge who comes between them and the sun
In a pillar of radiant house-dust.

xlvi

Mountain air from the mountain up behind;
Out front, the end-of-summer, stone-walled fields;
And in a slated house the fiddle going

Like a flat stone skimmed at sunset
Or the irrevocable slipstream of flat earth
Still fleeing behind space.

Was music once a proof of God's existence?
As long as it admits things beyond measure,
That supposition stands.

So let the ear attend like a farmhouse window
In placid light, where the extravagant
Passed once under full sail into the longed-for.

The visible sea at a distance from the shore
Or beyond the anchoring grounds
Was called the offing.

The emptier it stood, the more compelled
The eye that scanned it.
But once you turned your back on it, your back

Was suddenly all eyes like Argus's.
Then, when you'd look again, the offing felt
Untrespassed still, and yet somehow vacated

As if a lambent troop that exercised
On the borders of your vision had withdrawn
Behind the skyline to manoeuvre and regroup.

xlviii

Strange how things in the offing, once they're sensed,
Convert to things foreknown;
And how what's come upon is manifest

Only in light of what has been gone through.
Seventh heaven may be
The whole truth of a sixth sense come to pass.

At any rate, when light breaks over me
The way it did on the road beyond Coleraine
Where wind got saltier, the sky more hurried

And silver lame shivered on the Bann
Out in mid-channel between the painted poles,
That day I'll be in step with what escaped me.

The Crossing

(*Inferno*, Canto III, lines 82–129)

And there in a boat that came heading towards us
Was an old man, his hair snow-white with age,
Raging and bawling, 'Woe to you, wicked spirits!

O never hope to see the heavenly skies!
I come to bring you to the other shore,
To eternal darkness, to the fire and ice.

And you there, you, the living soul, separate
Yourself from these others who are dead.'
But when he saw that I did not stand aside

He said, 'By another way, by other harbours
You shall reach a different shore and pass over.
A lighter boat must be your carrier.'

And my guide said, 'Quiet your anger, Charon.
There where all can be done that has been willed
This has been willed; so there can be no question.'

Then straightaway he shut his grizzled jaws,
The ferryman of that livid marsh,
Who had wheels of fire flaming round his eyes.

But as soon as they had heard the cruel words,
Those lost souls, all naked and exhausted,
Changed their colour and their teeth chattered;

They blasphemed God and their parents on the earth,
The human race, the place and date and seedbed
Of their own begetting and of their birth,

Then all together, bitterly weeping, made
Their way towards the accursed shore that waits

For every man who does not fear his God.

The demon Charon's eyes are like hot coals fanned.
He beckons them and herds all of them in
And beats with his oar whoever drops behind.

As one by one the leaves fall off in autumn
Until at last the branch is bare and sees
All that was looted from it on the ground,

So the bad seed of Adam, at a signal
Pitch themselves off that shore one by one,
Each like a falcon answering its call.

They go away like this over the brown waters
And before they have landed on the other side
Upon this side once more a new crowd gathers.

'My son,' the courteous master said to me,
'All those who die under the wrath of God
Come together here from every country

And they are eager to go across the river
Because Divine Justice goads them with its spur
So that their fear is turned into desire.

No good spirits ever pass this way
And therefore, if Charon objects to you,
You should understand well what his words imply.'

The Spirit Level

For Helen Vendler

Contents

The Rain Stick

for Beth and Rand

Upend the rain stick and what happens next
Is a music that you never would have known
To listen for. In a cactus stalk

Downpour, sluice-rush, spillage and backwash
Come flowing through. You stand there like a pipe
Being played by water, you shake it again lightly

And diminuendo runs through all its scales
Like a gutter stopping trickling. And now here comes
A sprinkle of drops out of the freshened leaves,

Then subtle little wets off grass and daisies;
Then glitter-drizzle, almost-breaths of air.
Upend the stick again. What happens next

Is undiminished for having happened once,
Twice, ten, a thousand times before.
Who cares if all the music that transpires

Is the fall of grit or dry seeds through a cactus?
You are like a rich man entering heaven
Through the ear of a raindrop. Listen now again.

To a Dutch Potter in Ireland

for Sonja Landweer

Then I entered a strongroom of vocabulary
Where words like urns that had come through the fire
Stood in their bone-dry alcoves next a kiln

And came away changed, like the guard who'd seen
The stone move in a diamond-blaze of air
Or the gates of horn behind the gates of clay.

I

The soils I knew ran dirty. River sand
Was the one clean thing that stayed itself
In that slabbery, clabbery, wintry, puddled ground.

Until I found Bann clay. Like wet daylight
Or viscous satin under the felt and frieze
Of humus layers. The true diatomite

Discovered in a little sucky hole,
Grey-blue, dull-shining, scentless, touchable –
Like the earth's old ointment box, sticky and cool.

At that stage you were swimming in the sea
Or running from it, luminous with plankton,
A nymph of phosphor by the Norder Zee,

A vestal of the goddess Silica,
She who is under grass and glass and ash
In the fiery heartlands of Ceramica.

We might have known each other then, in that
Cold gleam-life under ground and off the water.
Weird twins of puddle, paddle, pit-a-pat,

And might have done the small forbidden things –
Worked at mud-pies or gone too high on swings,
Played 'secrets' in the hedge or 'touching tongues' –

But did not, in the terrible event.
Night after night instead, in the Netherlands,
You watched the bombers kill; then, heaven-sent,

Came backlit from the fire through war and wartime
And ever after, every blessed time,
Through glazes of fired quartz and iron and lime.

And if glazes, as you say, bring down the sun,
Your potter's wheel is bringing up the earth.
Hosannah ex infernis. Burning wells.

Hosannah in clean sand and kaolin
And, 'now that the rye crop waves beside the ruins',
In ash-pits, oxides, shards and chlorophylls.

2   After Liberation

i

Sheer, bright-shining spring, spring as it used to be,
Cold in the morning, but as broad daylight
Swings open, the everlasting sky
Is a marvel to survivors.

In a pearly clarity that bathes the fields
Things as they were come back; slow horses
Plough the fallow, war rumbles away
In the near distance.

To have lived it through and now be free to give
Utterance, body and soul – to wake and know
Every time that it's gone and gone for good, the thing

That nearly broke you –

Is worth it all, the five years on the rack,
The fighting back, the being resigned, and not
One of the unborn will appreciate
Freedom like this ever.

ii

Turning tides, their regularities!
What is the heart, that it ever was afraid,
Knowing as it must know spring's release,
Shining heart, heart constant as a tide?

Omnipresent, imperturbable
Is the life that death springs from.
And complaint is wrong, the slightest complaint at all,
Now that the rye crop waves beside the ruins.

from the Dutch of J. C. Bloem (1887-1966)

A Brigid's Girdle

for Adele

Last time I wrote I wrote from a rustic table
Under magnolias in South Carolina
As blossoms fell on me, and a white gable
As clean-lined as the prow of a white liner

Bisected sunlight in the sunlit yard.
I was glad of the early heat and the first quiet
I'd had for weeks. I heard the mocking bird
And a delicious, articulate

Flight of small plinkings from a dulcimer
Like feminine rhymes migrating to the north
Where you faced the music and the ache of summer
And earth's foreknowledge gathered in the earth.

Now it's St Brigid's Day and the first snowdrop
In County Wicklow, and this a Brigid's Girdle
I'm plaiting for you, an airy fairy hoop
(Like one of those old crinolines they'd trindle),

Twisted straw that's lifted in a circle
To handsel and to heal, a rite of spring
As strange and lightsome and traditional
As the motions you go through going through the thing.

Mint

It looked like a clump of small dusty nettles
Growing wild at the gable of the house
Beyond where we dumped our refuse and old bottles:
Unverdant ever, almost beneath notice.

But, to be fair, it also spelled promise
And newness in the back yard of our life
As if something callow yet tenacious
Sauntered in green alleys and grew rife.

The snip of scissor blades, the light of Sunday
Mornings when the mint was cut and loved:
My last things will be first things slipping from me.
Yet let all things go free that have survived.

Let the smells of mint go heady and defenceless
Like inmates liberated in that yard.
Like the disregarded ones we turned against
Because we'd failed them by our disregard.

A Sofa in the Forties

All of us on the sofa in a line, kneeling
Behind each other, eldest down to youngest,
Elbows going like pistons, for this was a train

And between the jamb-wall and the bedroom door
Our speed and distance were inestimable.
First we shunted, then we whistled, then

Somebody collected the invisible
For tickets and very gravely punched it
As carriage after carriage under us

Moved faster, *chooka-chook*, the sofa legs
Went giddy and the unreachable ones
Far out on the kitchen floor began to wave.

*

Ghost-train? Death-gondola? The carved, curved ends,
Black leatherette and ornate gauntness of it
Made it seem the sofa had achieved

Flotation. Its castors on tip-toe,
Its braid and fluent backboard gave it airs
Of superannuated pageantry:

When visitors endured it, straight-backed,
When it stood off in its own remoteness,
When the insufficient toys appeared on it

On Christmas mornings, it held out as itself,
Potentially heavenbound, earthbound for sure,
Among things that might add up or let you down.

*

We entered history and ignorance
Under the wireless shelf. *Yippee-i-ay*,
Sang 'The Riders of the Range'. HERE IS THE NEWS,

Said the absolute speaker. Between him and us
A great gulf was fixed where pronunciation
Reigned tyrannically. The aerial wire

Swept from a treetop down in through a hole
Bored in the windowframe. When it moved in wind,
The sway of language and its furtherings

Swept and swayed in us like nets in water
Or the abstract, lonely curve of distant trains
As we entered history and ignorance.

*

We occupied our seats with all our might,
Fit for the uncomfortableness.
Constancy was its own reward already.

Out in front, on the big upholstered arm,
Somebody craned to the side, driver or
Fireman, wiping his dry brow with the air

Of one who had run the gauntlet. We were
The last thing on his mind, it seemed; we sensed
A tunnel coming up where we'd pour through

Like unlit carriages through fields at night,
Our only job to sit, eyes straight ahead,
And be transported and make engine noise.

Keeping Going

for Hugh

The piper coming from far away is you
With a whitewash brush for a sporran
Wobbling round you, a kitchen chair
Upside down on your shoulder, your right arm
Pretending to tuck the bag beneath your elbow,
Your pop-eyes and big cheeks nearly bursting
With laughter, but keeping the drone going on
Interminably, between catches of breath.

*

The whitewash brush. An old blanched skirted thing
On the back of the byre door, biding its time
Until spring airs spelled lime in a work-bucket
And a potstick to mix it in with water.
Those smells brought tears to the eyes, we inhaled
A kind of greeny burning and thought of brimstone.
But the slop of the actual job
Of brushing walls, the watery grey
Being lashed on in broad swatches, then drying out
Whiter and whiter, all that worked like magic.
Where had we come from, what was this kingdom
We knew we'd been restored to? Our shadows
Moved on the wall and a tar border glittered
The full length of the house, a black divide
Like a freshly-opened, pungent, reeking trench.

*

Piss at the gable, the dead will congregate.
But separately. The women after dark,
Hunkering there a moment before bedtime,
The only time the soul was let alone,
The only time that face and body calmed

In the eye of heaven.
                              Buttermilk and urine,
The pantry, the housed beasts, the listening bedroom.
We were all together there in a foretime,
In a knowledge that might not translate beyond
Those wind-heaved midnights we still cannot be sure
Happened or not. It smelled of hill-fort clay
And cattle dung. When the thorn tree was cut down
You broke your arm. I shared the dread
When a strange bird perched for days on the byre roof.

                              *

That scene, with Macbeth helpless and desperate
In his nightmare – when he meets the hags again
And sees the apparitions in the pot –
I felt at home with that one all right. Hearth,
Steam and ululation, the smoky hair
Curtaining a cheek. 'Don't go near bad boys
In that college that you're bound for. Do you hear me?
Do you hear me speaking to you? Don't forget!'
And then the potstick quickening the gruel,
The steam crown swirled, everything intimate
And fear-swathed brightening for a moment,
Then going dull and fatal and away.

                              *

Grey matter like gruel flecked with blood
In spatters on the whitewash. A clean spot
Where his head had been, other stains subsumed
In the parched wall he leant his back against
That morning like any other morning,
Part-time reservist, toting his lunch-box.
A car came slow down Castle Street, made the halt,
Crossed the Diamond, slowed again and stopped
Level with him, although it was not his lift.
And then he saw an ordinary face

For what it was and a gun in his own face.
His right leg was hooked back, his sole and heel
Against the wall, his right knee propped up steady,
So he never moved, just pushed with all his might
Against himself, then fell past the tarred strip,
Feeding the gutter with his copious blood.

*

My dear brother, you have good stamina.
You stay on where it happens. Your big tractor
Pulls up at the Diamond, you wave at people,
You shout and laugh above the revs, you keep
Old roads open by driving on the new ones.
You called the piper's sporrans whitewash brushes
And then dressed up and marched us through the kitchen,
But you cannot make the dead walk or right wrong.
I see you at the end of your tether sometimes,
In the milking parlour, holding yourself up
Between two cows until your turn goes past,
Then coming to in the smell of dung again
And wondering, is this all? As it was
In the beginning, is now and shall be?
Then rubbing your eyes and seeing our old brush
Up on the byre door, and keeping going.

Two Lorries

It's raining on black coal and warm wet ashes.
There are tyre-marks in the yard, Agnew's old lorry
Has all its cribs down and Agnew the coalman
With his Belfast accent's sweet-talking my mother.
Would she ever go to a film in Magherafelt?
But it's raining and he still has half the load

To deliver farther on. This time the lode
Our coal came from was silk-black, so the ashes
Will be the silkiest white. The Magherafelt
(Via Toomebridge) bus goes by. The half-stripped lorry
With its emptied, folded coal-bags moves my mother:
The tasty ways of a leather-aproned coalman!

And films no less! The conceit of a coalman...
She goes back in and gets out the black lead
And emery paper, this nineteen-forties mother,
All business round her stove, half-wiping ashes
With a backhand from her cheek as the bolted lorry
Gets revved and turned and heads for Magherafelt

And the last delivery. Oh, Magherafelt!
Oh, dream of red plush and a city coalman
As time fastforwards and a different lorry
Groans into shot, up Broad Street, with a payload
That will blow the bus station to dust and ashes...
After that happened, I'd a vision of my mother,

A revenant on the bench where I would meet her
In that cold-floored waiting-room in Magherafelt,
Her shopping bags full up with shovelled ashes.
Death walked out past her like a dust-faced coalman
Refolding body-bags, plying his load
Empty upon empty, in a flurry

Of motes and engine-revs, but which lorry
Was it now? Young Agnew's or that other,
Heavier, deadlier one, set to explode
In a time beyond her time in Magherafelt...
So tally bags and sweet-talk darkness, coalman.
Listen to the rain spit in new ashes

As you heft a load of dust that was Magherafelt,
Then reappear from your lorry as my mother's
Dreamboat coalman filmed in silk-white ashes.

Damson

Gules and cement dust. A matte tacky blood
On the bricklayer's knuckles, like the damson stain
That seeped through his packed lunch.

                                    A full hod stood
Against the mortared wall, his big bright trowel
In his left hand (for once) was pointing down
As he marvelled at his right, held high and raw:
King of the castle, scaffold-stepper, shown
Bleeding to the world.

                        Wound that I saw
In glutinous colour fifty years ago –
Damson as omen, weird, a dream to read –
Is weeping with the held-at-arm's-length dead
From everywhere and nowhere, here and now.

                *

Over and over, the slur, the scrape and mix
As he trowelled and retrowelled and laid down
Courses of glum mortar. Then the bricks
Jiggled and settled, tocked and tapped in line.
I loved especially the trowel's shine,
Its edge and apex always coming clean
And brightening itself by mucking in.
It looked light but felt heavy as a weapon,
Yet when he lifted it there was no strain.
It was all point and skim and float and glisten
Until he washed and lapped it tight in sacking
Like a cult blade that had to be kept hidden.

                *

Ghosts with their tongues out for a lick of blood
Are crowding up the ladder, all unhealed,

And some of them still rigged in bloody gear.
Drive them back to the doorstep or the road
Where they lay in their own blood once, in the hot
Nausea and last gasp of dear life.
Trowel-wielder, woundie, drive them off
Like Odysseus in Hades lashing out
With his sword that dug the trench and cut the throat
Of the sacrificial lamb.
                         But not like him –
Builder, not sacker, your shield the mortar board –
Drive them back to the wine-dark taste of home,
The smell of damsons simmering in a pot,
Jam ladled thick and steaming down the sunlight.

Weighing In

The 56 lb. weight. A solid iron
Unit of negation. Stamped and cast
With an inset, rung-thick, moulded, short crossbar

For a handle. Squared-off and harmless-looking
Until you tried to lift it, then a socket-ripping,
Life-belittling force –

Gravity's black box, the immovable
Stamp and squat and square-root of dead weight.
Yet balance it

Against another one placed on a weighbridge –
On a well-adjusted, freshly greased weighbridge –
And everything trembled, flowed with give and take.

                    *

And this is all the good tidings amount to:
This principle of bearing, bearing up
And bearing out, just having to

Balance the intolerable in others
Against our own, having to abide
Whatever we settled for and settled into

Against our better judgement. Passive
Suffering makes the world go round.
Peace on earth, men of good will, all that

Holds good only as long as the balance holds,
The scales ride steady and the angels' strain
Prolongs itself at an unearthly pitch.

*

To refuse the other cheek. To cast the stone.
Not to do so some time, not to break with
The obedient one you hurt yourself into

Is to fail the hurt, the self, the ingrown rule.
Prophesy who struck thee! When soldiers mocked
Blindfolded Jesus and he didn't strike back

They were neither shamed nor edified, although
Something was made manifest – the power
Of power not exercised, of hope inferred

By the powerless forever. Still, for Jesus' sake,
Do me a favour, would you, just this once?
Prophesy, give scandal, cast the stone.

*

Two sides to every question, yes, yes, yes...
But every now and then, just weighing in
Is what it must come down to, and without

Any self-exculpation or self-pity.
Alas, one night when follow-through was called for
And a quick hit would have fairly rankled,

You countered that it was my narrowness
That kept me keen, so got a first submission.
I held back when I should have drawn blood

And that way (*mea culpa*) lost an edge.
A deep mistaken chivalry, old friend.
At this stage only foul play cleans the slate.

St Kevin and the Blackbird

And then there was St Kevin and the blackbird.
The saint is kneeling, arms stretched out, inside
His cell, but the cell is narrow, so

One turned-up palm is out the window, stiff
As a crossbeam, when a blackbird lands
And lays in it and settles down to nest.

Kevin feels the warm eggs, the small breast, the tucked
Neat head and claws and, finding himself linked
Into the network of eternal life,

Is moved to pity: now he must hold his hand
Like a branch out in the sun and rain for weeks
Until the young are hatched and fledged and flown.

*

And since the whole thing's imagined anyhow,
Imagine being Kevin. Which is he?
Self-forgetful or in agony all the time

From the neck on out down through his hurting forearms?
Are his fingers sleeping? Does he still feel his knees?
Or has the shut-eyed blank of underearth

Crept up through him? Is there distance in his head?
Alone and mirrored clear in love's deep river,
'To labour and not to seek reward,' he prays,

A prayer his body makes entirely
For he has forgotten self, forgotten bird
And on the riverbank forgotten the river's name.

The Flight Path

1

The first fold first, then more foldovers drawn
Tighter and neater every time until
The whole of the paper got itself reduced
To a pleated square he'd take up by two corners,
Then hold like a promise he had the power to break
But never did.
                    A dove rose in my breast
Every time my father's hands came clean
With a paper boat between them, ark in air,
The lines of it as taut as a pegged tent:
High-sterned, splay-bottomed, the little pyramid
At the centre every bit as hollow
As a part of me that sank because it knew
The whole thing would go soggy once you launched it.

2

Equal and opposite, the part that lifts
Into those *full-starred heavens that winter sees*
When I stand in Wicklow under the flight path
Of a late jet out of Dublin, its risen light
Winking ahead of what it hauls away:
Heavy engine noise and its abatement
Widening far back down, a wake through starlight.

The sycamore speaks in sycamore from darkness,
The light behind my shoulder's cottage lamplight.
I'm in the doorway early in the night,
Standing-in in myself for all of those
The stance perpetuates: the stay-at-homes
Who leant against the jamb and watched and waited,
The ones we learned to love by waving back at
Or coming towards again in different clothes

They were slightly shy of.
                              Who never once forgot
A name or a face, nor looked down suddenly
As the plane was reaching cruising altitude
To realize that the house they'd just passed over –
Too far back now to see – was the same house
They'd left an hour before, still kissing, kissing,
As the taxi driver loaded up the cases.

3

Up and away. The buzz from duty free.
Black velvet. Bourbon. Love letters on high.
The spacewalk of Manhattan. The re-entry.

Then California. Laid-back Tiburon.
Burgers at Sam's, deck-tables and champagne,
Plus a wall-eyed, hard-baked seagull looking on.

Again re-entry. Vows revowed. And off –
Reculer pour sauter, within one year of
Coming back, less long goodbye than stand-off.

So to Glanmore. Glanmore. Glanmore. Glanmore.
At bay, at one, at work, at risk and sure.
Covert and pad. Oak, bay and sycamore.

Jet-sitting next. Across and across and across.
Westering, eastering, the jumbo a school bus,
'The Yard' a cross between the farm and campus,

A holding pattern and a tautening purchase –
Sweeney astray in home truths out of Horace:
Skies change, not cares, for those who cross the seas.

4

The following for the record, in the light

Of everything before and since:
One bright May morning, nineteen-seventy-nine,
Just off the red-eye special from New York,
I'm on the train for Belfast. Plain, simple
Exhilaration at being back: the sea
At Skerries, the nuptial hawthorn bloom,
The trip north taking sweet hold like a chain
On every bodily sprocket.
                                    Enter then –
As if he were some *film noir* border guard –
Enter this one I'd last met in a dream,
More grimfaced now than in the dream itself
When he'd flagged me down at the side of a mountain road,
Come up and leant his elbow on the roof
And explained through the open window of the car
That all I'd have to do was drive a van
Carefully in to the next customs post
At Pettigo, switch off, get out as if
I were on my way with dockets to the office –
But then instead I'd walk ten yards more down
Towards the main street and get in with – here
Another schoolfriend's name, a wink and smile,
I'd know him all right, he'd be in a Ford
And I'd be home in three hours' time, as safe
As houses...
                        So he enters and sits down
Opposite and goes for me head on.
'When, for fuck's sake, are you going to write
Something for us?' 'If I do write something,
Whatever it is, I'll be writing for myself.'
And that was that. Or words to that effect.

The gaol walls all those months were smeared with shite.
Out of Long Kesh after his dirty protest
The red eyes were the eyes of Ciaran Nugent
Like something out of Dante's scurfy hell,
Drilling their way through the rhymes and images
Where I too walked behind the righteous Virgil,

As safe as houses and translating freely:
When he had said all this, his eyes rolled
And his teeth, like a dog's teeth clamping round a bone,
Bit into the skull and again took hold.

5

When I answered that I came from 'far away',
The policeman at the roadblock snapped, 'Where's that?'
He'd only half heard what I said and thought
It was the name of some place up the country.

And now it is – both where I have been living
And where I left – a distance still to go
Like starlight that is light years on the go
From far away and takes light years arriving.

6

Out of the blue then, the sheer exaltation
Of remembering climbing zig-zag up warm steps
To the hermit's eyrie above Rocamadour.
Crows sailing high and close, a lizard pulsing
On gravel at my feet, its front legs set
Like the jointed front struts of a moon vehicle.
And bigly, softly as the breath of life
In a breath of air, a lime-green butterfly
Crossing the pilgrims' sunstruck *via crucis.*

Eleven in the morning. I made a note:
'Rock-lover, loner, sky-sentry, all hail!'
And somewhere the dove rose. And kept on rising.

An Invocation

Incline to me, MacDiarmid, out of Shetland,
Stone-eyed from stone-gazing, sobered up
And thrawn. Not the old vigilante

Of the chimney corner, having us on,
Setting us off, the drinkers' drinker; no,
Incline as the sage of winds that flout the rock face,

As gull stalled in the sea breeze, gatekeeper
Of the open gates behind the brows of birds –
Not to hear me take back smart remarks

About your MacGonagallish propensities –
For I do not – but I add in middle age:
I underprized your far-out, blathering genius.

*

Those years in the shore-view house, especially.
More intellectual billygoat than scapegoat,
Beyond the stony limits, writing-mad.

That pride of being tested. Of solitude.
Your big pale forehead in the window glass
Like the earth's curve on the sea's curve to the north.

At your wits' end then, always on the go
To the beach and back, taking heady bearings
Between the horizon and the dictionary,

Hard-liner on the rock face of the old
Questions and answers, to which I add my own:
'Who is my neighbour? My neighbour is all mankind.'

*

And if you won't incline, endure
At an embraced distance. Be the wee
Contrary stormcock that you always were,

The weather-eye of a poetry like the weather,
A shifting force, a factor factored in
Whether it prevails or not, constantly

A function of its time and place
And sometimes of our own. Never, at any rate,
Beyond us, even when outlandish.

In the accent, in the idiom, in
The idea like a thistle in the wind,
A catechism worth repeating always.

Hugh MacDiarmid 1892-1978

Mycenae Lookout

The ox is on my tongue

Aeschylus, *Agamemnon*

1 *The Watchman's War*

Some people wept, and not for sorrow – joy
That the king had armed and upped and sailed for Troy,
But inside me like struck sound in a gong
That killing-fest, the life-warp and world-wrong
It brought to pass, still augured and endured.
I'd dream of blood in bright webs in a ford,
Of bodies raining down like tattered meat
On top of me asleep – and me the lookout
The queen's command had posted and forgotten,
The blind spot her farsightedness relied on.
And then the ox would lurch against the gong
And deaden it and I would feel my tongue
Like the dropped gangplank of a cattle truck,
Trampled and rattled, running piss and muck,
All swimmy-trembly as the lick of fire,
A victory beacon in an abattoir...
Next thing then I would waken at a loss,
For all the world a sheepdog stretched in grass,
Exposed to what I knew, still honour-bound
To concentrate attention out beyond
The city and the border, on that line
Where the blaze would leap the hills when Troy had fallen.

My sentry work was fate, a home to go to,
An in-between-times that I had to row through
Year after year: when the mist would start
To lift off fields and inlets, when morning light
Would open like the grain of light being split,
Day in, day out, I'd come alive again,

Silent and sunned as an esker on a plain,
Up on my elbows, gazing, biding time
In my outpost on the roof...What was to come
Out of that ten years' wait that was the war
Flawed the black mirror of my frozen stare.
If a god of justice had reached down from heaven
For a strong beam to hang his scale-pans on
He would have found me tensed and ready-made.
I balanced between destiny and dread
And saw it coming, clouds bloodshot with the red
Of victory fires, the raw wound of that dawn
Igniting and erupting, bearing down
Like lava on a fleeing population...
Up on my elbows, head back, shutting out
The agony of Clytemnestra's love-shout
That rose through the palace like the yell of troops
Hurled by King Agamemnon from the ships.

2   *Cassandra*

No such thing
as innocent
bystanding.

Her soiled vest,
her little breasts,
her clipped, devast-

ated, scabbed
punk head,
the char-eyed

famine gawk –
she looked
camp-fucked

and simple.
People
could feel

a missed
trueness in them
focus,

a homecoming
in her dropped-wing,
half-calculating

bewilderment.
No such thing
as innocent.

Old King Cock-
of-the-Walk
was back,

King Kill-
the-Child-
and-Take-

What-Comes,
King Agamem-
non's drum-

balled, old buck's
stride was back.
And then her Greek

words came,
a lamb
at lambing time,

bleat of clair-
voyant dread,

the gene-hammer

and tread
of the roused god.
And a result-

ant shock desire
in bystanders
to do it to her

there and then.
Little rent
cunt of their guilt:

in she went
to the knife,
to the killer wife,

to the net over
her and her slaver,
the Troy reaver,

saying, 'A wipe
of the sponge,
that's it.

The shadow-hinge
swings unpredict-
ably and the light's

blanked out.'

3   *His Dawn Vision*

Cities of grass. Fort walls. The dumbstruck palace.
I'd come to with the night wind on my face,

Agog, alert again, but far, far less

Focused on victory than I should have been –
Still isolated in my old disdain
Of claques who always needed to be seen

And heard as the true Argives. Mouth athletes,
Quoting the oracle and quoting dates,
Petitioning, accusing, taking votes.

No element that should have carried weight
Out of the grievous distance would translate.
Our war stalled in the pre-articulate.

The little violets' heads bowed on their stems,
The pre-dawn gossamers, all dew and scrim
And star-lace, it was more through them

I felt the beating of the huge time-wound
We lived inside. My soul wept in my hand
When I would touch them, my whole being rained

Down on myself, I saw cities of grass,
Valleys of longing, tombs, a wind-swept brightness,
And far-off, in a hilly, ominous place,

Small crowds of people watching as a man
Jumped a fresh earth-wall and another ran
Amorously, it seemed, to strike him down.

4   *The Nights*

They both needed to talk,
pretending what they needed
was my advice. Behind backs
each one of them confided

it was sexual overload
every time they did it —
and indeed from the beginning
(a child could have hardly missed it)
their real life was the bed.

The king should have been told,
but who was there to tell him
if not myself? I willed them
to cease and break the hold
of my cross-purposed silence
but still kept on, all smiles
to Aegisthus every morning,
much favoured and self-loathing.
The roof was like an eardrum.

The ox's tons of dumb
inertia stood, head-down
and motionless as a herm.
Atlas, watchmen's patron,
would come into my mind,
the only other one
up at all hours, ox-bowed
under his yoke of cloud
out there at the world's end.

The loft-floor where the gods
and goddesses took lovers
and made out endlessly
successfully, those thuds
and moans through the cloud cover
were wholly on his shoulders.
Sometimes I thought of us
apotheosized to boulders
called Aphrodite's Pillars.

High and low in those days
hit their stride together.

When the captains in the horse
felt Helen's hand caress
its wooden boards and belly
they nearly rode each other.
But in the end Troy's mothers
bore their brunt in alley,
bloodied cot and bed.
The war put all men mad,
horned, horsed or roof-posted,
the boasting and the bested.

My own mind was a bull-pen
where horned King Agamemnon
had stamped his weight in gold.
But when hills broke into flame
and the queen wailed on and came,
it was the king I sold.
I moved beyond bad faith:
for his bullion bars, his bonus
was a rope-net and a blood-bath.
And the peace had come upon us.

5   *His Reverie of Water*

At Troy, at Athens, what I most clearly
see and nearly smell
is the fresh water.

A filled bath, still unentered
and unstained, waiting behind housewalls
that the far cries of the butchered on the plain

keep dying into, until the hero comes
surging in incomprehensibly
to be attended to and be alone,

stripped to the skin, blood-plastered, moaning
and rocking, splashing, dozing off,
accommodated as if he were a stranger.

And the well at Athens too.
Or rather that old lifeline leading up
and down from the Acropolis

to the well itself, a set of timber steps
slatted in between the sheer cliff face
and a free-standing, covering spur of rock,

secret staircase the defenders knew
and the invaders found, where what was to be
Greek met Greek,

the ladder of the future
and the past, besieger and besieged,
the treadmill of assault

turned waterwheel, the rungs of stealth
and habit all the one
bare foot extended, searching.

And then this ladder of our own that ran
deep into a well-shaft being sunk
in broad daylight, men puddling at the source

through tawny mud, then coming back up
deeper in themselves for having been there,
like discharged soldiers testing the safe ground,

finders, keepers, seers of fresh water
in the bountiful round mouths of iron pumps
and gushing taps.

for Cynthia and Dmitri Hadzi

The First Words

The first words got polluted
Like river water in the morning
Flowing with the dirt
Of blurbs and the front pages.
My only drink is meaning from the deep brain,
What the birds and the grass and the stones drink.
Let everything flow
Up to the four elements,
Up to water and earth and fire and air.

from the Romanian of Marin Sorescu

The Gravel Walks

River gravel. In the beginning, that.
High summer, and the angler's motorbike
Deep in roadside flowers, like a fallen knight
Whose ghost we'd lately questioned: 'Any luck?'

As the engines of the world prepared, green nuts
Dangled and clustered closer to the whirlpool.
The trees dipped down. The flints and sandstone-bits
Worked themselves smooth and smaller in a sparkle

Of shallow, hurrying barley-sugar water
Where minnows schooled that we scared when we played –
An eternity that ended once a tractor
Dropped its link-box in the gravel bed

And cement mixers began to come to life
And men in dungarees, like captive shades,
Mixed concrete, loaded, wheeled, turned, wheeled, as if
The Pharaoh's brickyards burned inside their heads.

*

Hoard and praise the verity of gravel.
Gems for the undeluded. Milt of earth.
Its plain, champing song against the shovel
Soundtests and sandblasts words like 'honest worth'.

Beautiful in or out of the river,
The kingdom of gravel was inside you too –
Deep down, far back, clear water running over
Pebbles of caramel, hailstone, mackerel-blue.

But the actual washed stuff kept you slow and steady
As you went stooping with your barrow full

Into an absolution of the body,
The shriven life tired bones and marrow feel.

So walk on air against your better judgement
Establishing yourself somewhere in between
Those solid batches mixed with grey cement
And a tune called 'The Gravel Walks' that conjures green.

Whitby-sur-Moyola

Caedmon too I was lucky to have known,
Back *in situ* there with his full bucket
And armfuls of clean straw, the perfect yardman,
Unabsorbed in what he had to do
But doing it perfectly, and watching you.
He had worked his angel stint. He was hard as nails
And all that time he'd been poeting with the harp
His real gift was the big ignorant roar
He could still let out of him, just bogging in
As if the sacred subjects were a herd
That had broken out and needed rounding up.
I never saw him once with his hands joined
Unless it was a case of eyes to heaven
And the quick sniff and test of fingertips
After he'd passed them through a sick beast's water.
Oh, Caedmon was the real thing all right.

The Thimble

1

In the House of Carnal Murals
The painter used it to hold a special red
He touched the lips and freshest bite-marks with.

2

Until the Reformation, it was revered
As a relic of St Adaman.
The workers in a certain foundry cast
A bell, so heavy, it was said,
No apparatus could lift it to the belltower –
And afterwards were stricken one by one
With a kind of sleeping sickness.
In the middle of the fiery delirium
Of metal pouring, they would all fall quiet
And see green waterweed and stepping stones
Across the molten bronze.
So Adaman arrived and blessed their hands
And eyes and cured them, but at that hour
The bell too shrank miraculously
And henceforth was known to the faithful
And registered in the canons' inventory
As Adaman's Thimble.

3

Was this the measure of the sweetest promise,
The dipped thirst-brush, the dew of paradise
That would flee my tongue when they said 'A thimbleful'?

4

Now a teenager
With shaved head
And translucent shoulders
Wears it for a nipple-cap.

5

And so on.

The Butter-Print

Who carved on the butter-print's round open face
A cross-hatched head of rye, all jags and bristles?
Why should soft butter bear that sharp device
As if its breast were scored with slivered glass?

When I was small I swallowed an awn of rye.
My throat was like standing crop probed by a scythe.
I felt the edge slide and the point stick deep
Until, when I coughed and coughed and coughed it up,

My breathing came dawn-cold, so clear and sudden
I might have been inhaling airs from heaven
Where healed and martyred Agatha stares down
At the relic knife as I stared at the awn.

Remembered Columns

The solid letters of the world grew airy.
The marble serifs, the clearly blocked uprights
Built upon rocks and set upon the heights
Rose like remembered columns in a story

About the Virgin's house that rose and flew
And landed on the hilltop at Loreto.
I lift my eyes in a light-headed credo,
Discovering what survives translation true.

'Poet's Chair'

for Carolyn Mulholland

Leonardo said: the sun has never
Seen a shadow. Now watch the sculptor move
Full circle round her next work, like a lover
In the sphere of shifting angles and fixed love.

1

Angling shadows of itself are what
Your 'Poet's Chair' stands to and rises out of
In its sun-stalked inner-city courtyard.
On the *qui vive* all the time, its four legs land
On their feet – catsfoot, goatfoot, big soft splay-foot too;
Its straight back sprouts two bronze and leafy saplings.
Every flibbertigibbet in the town,
Old birds and boozers, late-night pissers, kissers,
All have a go at sitting on it some time.
It's the way the air behind them's winged and full,
The way a graft has seized their shoulder-blades
That makes them happy. Once out of nature,
They're going to come back in leaf and bloom
And angel step. Or something like that. *Leaves*
On a bloody chair! Would you believe it?

2

Next thing I see the chair in a white prison
With Socrates sitting on it, bald as a coot,
Discoursing in bright sunlight with his friends.
His time is short. The day his trial began
A verdant boat sailed from Apollo's shrine
In Delos, for the annual rite
Of commemoration. Until its wreathed
And creepered rigging re-enters Athens

Harbour, the city's life is holy.
No executions. No hemlock bowl. No tears
And none now as the poison does its work
And the expert jailer talks the company through
The stages of the numbness. Socrates
At the centre of the city and the day
Has proved the soul immortal. The bronze leaves
Cannot believe their ears, it is so silent.
Soon Crito will have to close his eyes and mouth,
But for the moment everything's an ache
Deferred, foreknown, imagined and most real.

3

My father's ploughing one, two, three, four sides
Of the lea ground where I sit all-seeing
At centre field, my back to the thorn tree
They never cut. The horses are all hoof
And burnished flank, I am all foreknowledge.
Of the poem as a ploughshare that turns time
Up and over. Of the chair in leaf
The fairy thorn is entering for the future.
Of being here for good in every sense.

The Swing

Fingertips just tipping you would send you
Every bit as far – once you got going –
As a big push in the back.
                             Sooner or later,
We all learned one by one to go sky high,
Backward and forward in the open shed,
Toeing and rowing and jackknifing through air.

                  *

Not Fragonard. Nor Brueghel. It was more
Hans Memling's light of heaven off green grass,
Light over fields and hedges, the shed-mouth
Sunstruck and expectant, the bedding-straw
Piled to one side, like a nativity
Foreground and background waiting for the figures.
And then, in the middle ground, the swing itself
With an old lopsided sack in the loop of it,
Perfectly still, hanging like pulley-slack,
A lure let down to tempt the soul to rise.

                  *

Even so, we favoured the earthbound. She
Sat there as majestic as an empress
Steeping her swollen feet one at a time
In the enamel basin, feeding it
Every now and again with an opulent
Steaming arc from a kettle on the floor
Beside her. The plout of that was music
To our ears, her smile a mitigation.
Whatever light the goddess had once shone
Around her favourite coming from the bath
Was what was needed then: there should have been

Fresh linen, ministrations by attendants,
Procession and amazement. Instead, she took
Each rolled elastic stocking and drew it on
Like the life she would not fail and was not
Meant for. And once, when she'd scoured the basin,
She came and sat to please us on the swing,
Neither out of place nor in her element,
Just tempted by it for a moment only,
Half-retrieving something half-confounded.
Instinctively we knew to let her be.

               *

To start up by yourself, you hitched the rope
Against your backside and backed on into it
Until it tautened, then tiptoed and drove off
As hard as possible. You hurled a gathered thing
From the small of your own back into the air.
Your head swept low, you heard the whole shed creak.

               *

We all learned one by one to go sky high.
Then townlands vanished into aerodromes,
Hiroshima made light of human bones,
Concorde's neb migrated towards the future.
So who were we to want to hang back there
In spite of all?
               In spite of all, we sailed
Beyond ourselves and over and above
The rafters aching in our shoulderblades,
The give and take of branches in our arms.

The Poplar

Wind shakes the big poplar, quicksilvering
The whole tree in a single sweep.
What bright scale fell and left this needle quivering?
What loaded balances have come to grief?

Two Stick Drawings

1

Claire O'Reilly used her granny's stick –
A crook-necked one – to snare the highest briars
That always grew the ripest blackberries.
When it came to gathering, Persephone
Was in the halfpenny place compared to Claire.
She'd trespass and climb gates and walk the railway
Where sootflakes blew into convolvulus
And the train tore past with the stoker yelling
Like a balked king from his iron chariot.

2

With its drover's canes and blackthorns and ash plants,
The ledge of the back seat of my father's car
Had turned into a kind of stick-shop window,
But the only one who ever window-shopped
Was Jim of the hanging jaw, for Jim was simple
And rain or shine he'd make his desperate rounds
From windscreen to back window, hands held up
To both sides of his face, peering and groaning.
So every now and then the sticks would be
Brought out for him and stood up one by one
Against the front mudguard; and one by one
Jim would take the measure of them, sight
And wield and slice and poke and parry
The unhindering air; until he found
The true extension of himself in one
That made him jubilant. He'd run and crow,
Stooped forward, with his right elbow stuck out
And the stick held horizontal to the ground,
Angled across in front of him, as if
He were leashed to it and it drew him on
Like a harness rod of the inexorable.

A Call

'Hold on,' she said, 'I'll just run out and get him.
The weather here's so good, he took the chance
To do a bit of weeding.'
                              So I saw him
Down on his hands and knees beside the leek rig,
Touching, inspecting, separating one
Stalk from the other, gently pulling up
Everything not tapered, frail and leafless,
Pleased to feel each little weed-root break,
But rueful also...

                      Then found myself listening to
The amplified grave ticking of hall clocks
Where the phone lay unattended in a calm
Of mirror glass and sunstruck pendulums...

And found myself then thinking: if it were nowadays,
This is how Death would summon Everyman.

Next thing he spoke and I nearly said I loved him.

The Errand

'On you go now! Run, son, like the devil
And tell your mother to try
To find me a bubble for the spirit level
And a new knot for this tie.'

But still he was glad, I know, when I stood my ground,
Putting it up to him
With a smile that trumped his smile and his fool's errand,
Waiting for the next move in the game.

A Dog Was Crying Tonight in Wicklow Also

in memory of Donatus Nwoga

When human beings found out about death
They sent the dog to Chukwu with a message:
They wanted to be let back to the house of life.
They didn't want to end up lost forever
Like burnt wood disappearing into smoke
Or ashes that get blown away to nothing.
Instead, they saw their souls in a flock at twilight
Cawing and headed back for the same old roosts
And the same bright airs and wing-stretchings each morning.
Death would be like a night spent in the wood:
At first light they'd be back in the house of life.
(The dog was meant to tell all this to Chukwu).

But death and human beings took second place
When he trotted off the path and started barking
At another dog in broad daylight just barking
Back at him from the far bank of a river.

And that is how the toad reached Chukwu first,
The toad who'd overheard in the beginning
What the dog was meant to tell. 'Human beings,' he said
(And here the toad was trusted absolutely),
'Human beings want death to last forever.'

Then Chukwu saw the people's souls in birds
Coming towards him like black spots off the sunset
To a place where there would be neither roosts nor trees
Nor any way back to the house of life.
And his mind reddened and darkened all at once
And nothing that the dog would tell him later
Could change that vision. Great chiefs and great loves
In obliterated light, the toad in mud,
The dog crying out all night behind the corpse house.

M.

When the deaf phonetician spread his hand
Over the dome of a speaker's skull
He could tell which diphthong and which vowel
By the bone vibrating to the sound.

A globe stops spinning. I set my palm
On a contour cold as permafrost
And imagine axle-hum and the steadfast
Russian of Osip Mandelstam.

An Architect

He fasted on the doorstep of his gift,
Exacting more, minding the boulder
And the raked zen gravel. But no slouch either

Whenever it came to whiskey, whether to
Lash into it or just to lash it out.
Courtly always, and rapt, and astonishing,

Like the day on the beach when he stepped out of his clothes
And waded along beside us in his pelt
Speculating, intelligent and lanky,

Taking things in his Elysian stride,
Talking his way back into sites and truths
The art required and his life came down to:

Blue slate and whitewash, shadow-lines, projections,
Things at once apparent and transparent,
Clean-edged, fine-drawn, drawn-out, redrawn, remembered...

Exit now, in his tweeds, down an aisle between
Drawing boards as far as the eye can see
To where it can't until he sketches where.

The Sharping Stone

In an apothecary's chest of drawers,
Sweet cedar that we'd purchased second hand,
In one of its weighty deep-sliding recesses
I found the sharping stone that was to be
Our gift to him. Still in its wrapping paper.
Like a baton of black light I'd failed to pass.

*

Airless cinder-depths. But all the same,
The way it lay there, it wakened something too...
I thought of us that evening on the logs,
Flat on our backs, the pair of us, parallel,
Supported head to heel, arms straight, eyes front,
Listening to the rain drip off the trees
And saying nothing, braced to the damp bark.
What possessed us? The bare, lopped loveliness
Of those two winter trunks, the way they seemed
Prepared for launching, at right angles across
A causeway of short fence-posts set like rollers.
Neither of us spoke. The puddles waited.
The workers had gone home, saws fallen silent.
And next thing down we lay, babes in the wood,
Gazing up at the flood-face of the sky
Until it seemed a flood was carrying us
Out of the forest park, feet first, eyes front,
Out of November, out of middle age,
Together, out, across the Sea of Moyle.

*

Sarcophage des époux. In terra cotta.
Etruscan couple shown side by side,
Recumbent on left elbows, husband pointing

With his right arm and watching where he points,
Wife in front, her earrings in, her braids
Down to her waist, taking her sexual ease.
He is all eyes, she is all brow and dream,
Her right forearm and hand held out as if
Some bird she sees in her deep inward gaze
Might be about to roost there. Domestic
Love, the artist thought, warm tones and property,
The frangibility of terra cotta...
Which is how they figured on the colour postcard
(*Louvre, Département des Antiquités*)
That we'd sent him once, then found among his things.

*

He loved inspired mistakes: his Spanish grandson's
English transliteration, thanking him
For a boat trip: 'That was a marvellous
Walk on the water, granddad.' And indeed
He walked on air himself, never more so
Than when he had been widowed and the youth
In him, the athlete who had wooed her –
Breasting tapes and clearing the high bars –
Grew lightsome once again. Going at eighty
On the bendiest roads, going for broke
At every point-to-point and poker-school,
'He commenced his wild career' a second time
And not a bother on him. Smoked like a train
And took the power mower in his stride.
Flirted and vaunted. Set fire to his bed.
Fell from a ladder. Learned to microwave.

*

So set the drawer on freshets of thaw water
And place the unused sharping stone inside it:
To be found next summer on a riverbank
Where scythes once hung all night in alder trees

And mowers played dawn scherzos on the blades,
Their arms like harpists' arms, one drawing towards,
One sweeping the bright rim of the extreme.

The Strand

The dotted line my father's ashplant made
On Sandymount Strand
Is something else the tide won't wash away.

The Walk

Glamoured the road, the day, and him and her
And everywhere they took me. When we stepped out
Cobbles were riverbed, the Sunday air
A high stream-roof that moved in silence over
Rhododendrons in full bloom, foxgloves
And hemlock, robin-run-the-hedge, the hedge
With its deckled ivy and thick shadows –
Until the riverbed itself appeared,
Gravelly, shallowy, summery with pools,
And made a world rim that was not for crossing.
Love brought me that far by the hand, without
The slightest doubt or irony, dry-eyed
And knowledgeable, contrary as be damned;
Then just kept standing there, not letting go.

*

So here is another longshot. Black and white.
A negative this time, in dazzle-dark,
Smudge and pallor where we make out you and me,
The selves we struggled with and struggled out of,
Two shades who have consumed each other's fire,
Two flames in sunlight that can sear and singe,
But seem like wisps of enervated air,
After-wavers, feathery ether-shifts...
Yet apt still to rekindle suddenly
If we find along the way charred grass and sticks
And an old fire-fragrance lingering on,
Erotic woodsmoke, witchery, intrigue,
Leaving us none the wiser, just better primed
To speed the plough again and feed the flame.

At the Wellhead

Your songs, when you sing them with your two eyes closed
As you always do, are like a local road
We've known every turn of in the past –
That midge-veiled, high-hedged side-road where you stood
Looking and listening until a car
Would come and go and leave you lonelier
Than you had been to begin with. So, sing on,
Dear shut-eyed one, dear far-voiced veteran,

Sing yourself to where the singing comes from,
Ardent and cut off like our blind neighbour
Who played the piano all day in her bedroom.
Her notes came out to us like hoisted water
Ravelling off a bucket at the wellhead
Where next thing we'd be listening, hushed and awkward.

*

That blind-from-birth, sweet-voiced, withdrawn musician
Was like a silver vein in heavy clay.
Night water glittering in the light of day.
But also just our neighbour, Rosie Keenan.
She touched our cheeks. She let us touch her braille
In books like books wallpaper patterns came in.
Her hands were active and her eyes were full
Of open darkness and a watery shine.
She knew us by our voices. She'd say she 'saw'
Whoever or whatever. Being with her
Was intimate and helpful, like a cure
You didn't notice happening. When I read
A poem with Keenan's well in it, she said,
'I can see the sky at the bottom of it now.'

At Banagher

Then all of a sudden there appears to me
The journeyman tailor who was my antecedent:
Up on a table, cross-legged, ripping out

A garment he must recut or resew,
His lips tight back, a thread between his teeth,
Keeping his counsel always, giving none,

His eyelids steady as wrinkled horn or iron.
Self-absenting, both migrant and ensconced;
Admitted into kitchens, into clothes

His touch has the power to turn to cloth again –
All of a sudden he appears to me,
Unopen, unmendacious, unillumined.

*

So more power to him on the job there, ill at ease
Under my scrutiny in spite of years
Of being inscrutable as he threaded needles

Or matched the facings, linings, hems and seams.
He holds the needle just off centre, squinting,
And licks the thread and licks and sweeps it through,

Then takes his time to draw both ends out even,
Plucking them sharply twice. Then back to stitching.
Does he ever question what it all amounts to

Or ever will? Or care where he lays his head?
My Lord Buddha of Banagher, the way
Is opener for your being in it.

Tollund

That Sunday morning we had travelled far.
We stood a long time out in Tollund Moss:
The low ground, the swart water, the thick grass
Hallucinatory and familiar.

A path through Jutland fields. Light traffic sound.
Willow bushes; rushes; bog-fir grags
In a swept and gated farmyard; dormant quags.
And silage under wraps in its silent mound.

It could have been a still out of the bright
'Townland of Peace', that poem of dream farms
Outside all contention. The scarecrow's arms
Stood open opposite the satellite

Dish in the paddock, where a standing stone
Had been resituated and landscaped,
With tourist signs in *futhark* runic script
In Danish and in English. Things had moved on.

It could have been Mulhollandstown or Scribe.
The byroads had their names on them in black
And white; it was user-friendly outback
Where we stood footloose, at home beyond the tribe,

More scouts than strangers, ghosts who'd walked abroad
Unfazed by light, to make a new beginning
And make a go of it, alive and sinning,
Ourselves again, free-willed again, not bad.

September 1994

Postscript

And some time make the time to drive out west
Into County Clare, along the Flaggy Shore,
In September or October, when the wind
And the light are working off each other
So that the ocean on one side is wild
With foam and glitter, and inland among stones
The surface of a slate-grey lake is lit
By the earthed lightning of a flock of swans,
Their feathers roughed and ruffling, white on white,
Their fully grown headstrong-looking heads
Tucked or cresting or busy underwater.
Useless to think you'll park and capture it
More thoroughly. You are neither here nor there,
A hurry through which known and strange things pass
As big soft buffetings come at the car sideways
And catch the heart off guard and blow it open.

Notes and Acknowledgements

Acknowledgements are due to the editors of the following magazines where these poems first appeared: *Agenda, Agni, Antaeus, College Green, Gown, The Guardian, Harvard Review, Honest Ulsterman, Independent on Sunday, The Irish Times, London Review of Books, Mica, The New Republic, New Welsh Review, Notre Dame Review, Oxford Poetry, Parnassus, Poetry, Poetry & Audience, Poetry Ireland Review, P. N. Review, Soho Square, The Southern Review, Thinker Review, Threepenny Review, TickleAce, Times Literary Supplement, Verse, Verso.* 'At the Wellhead', 'Keeping Going', 'The Sharping Stone' and section 5 of 'The Flight Path' were published in *The New Yorker*.

'The Flight Path' originally appeared *in P.N Review 88*, a special issue celebrating Donald Davie's seventieth birthday. It is published here in memory of Donald Davie, who died in 1995.

'After Liberation' first appeared in *Turning Tides* (Story Line Press, 1994); 'The First Words' is a version of a poem by Marin Sorescu from a translation by Ioana Russell-Gebbett (previously printed in *The Biggest Egg in the World*, Bloodaxe, 1987).

Seeing Things by SEAMUS HEANEY
First published in 1991
The Spirit Level by SEAMUS HEANEY
First published in 1996
This edition arranged with Faber and Faber Ltd. through Big Apple Agency, Inc.,
Labuan, Malaysia
Simplified Chinese edition copyright © 2024 Guangxi Normal University Press Group
Co., Ltd.

著作权合同登记号桂图登字:20 - 2024 - 003 号

图书在版编目(CIP)数据

幻视;酒精水准仪:汉、英/(爱尔兰)谢默斯·希尼著;朱玉
译. —桂林:广西师范大学出版社,2024.5
　(文学纪念碑)
　书名原文:Seeing Things/The Spirit Level
　ISBN 978 - 7 - 5598 - 6935 - 7

Ⅰ.①幻… Ⅱ.①谢… ②朱… Ⅲ.①诗集-爱尔兰-现代-
汉、英 Ⅳ.①I562.25

中国国家版本馆 CIP 数据核字(2024)第 093505 号

幻视·酒精水准仪:汉、英
HUANSHI·JIUJING SHUIZHUNYI:HAN、YING

出 品 人:刘广汉　　策　划:魏　东　　责任编辑:魏　东　程卫平
助理编辑:钟雨晴　　装帧设计:赵　瑾
广西师范大学出版社出版发行
（广西桂林市五里店路9号　　邮政编码:541004
　网址:http://www.bbtpress.com　　　　　　　　）
出版人:黄轩庄
全国新华书店经销
销售热线:021-65200318　021-31260822-898
山东临沂新华印刷物流集团有限责任公司印刷
(临沂高新技术产业开发区新华路1号　邮政编码:276017)
开本:889 mm×1 194 mm　　1/32
印张:13　　　　　字数:367 千
2024 年 5 月第 1 版　　2024 年 5 月第 1 次印刷
定价:78.00 元

如发现印装质量问题,影响阅读,请与出版社发行部门联系调换。